Amelia shook her head back and forth. This couldn't be happening.

"No contraception is one hundred percent assured. It seems this is an instance of..." Dr. Moretti looked between Amelia and Alessandro as if trying to gauge the appropriate word, and decided it didn't need clarifying. "You will want to visit your own doctor when you get home."

Home. A flat she shared with her sister. A sister still hell-bent on vengeance against her baby's father and cousin once removed. She pressed her fingers to her mouth, trying to keep the swell of nausea down. It was all too much.

She glanced up at the doctor and then to Alessandro, who looked as pale and shocked as she felt.

Moretti, realizing that there was clearly much to be discussed, announced that he would let himself out and left the two of them alone in a room that suddenly felt stifling. Alessandro collapsed back into the chair she had found him in that very morning only a few hours ago, when the world had been completely different.

When she wasn't carrying her enemy's baby.

A Billion-Dollar Revenge

Revenge is best served...red hot!

Ten years ago, the lives of Issy and Amelia were ruined by Gianni and Alessandro Rossi. Ever since, the Seymore sisters have plotted their revenge against the Italian billionaires. Now, it's time for Issy and Amelia to put their plan into action!

Innocent Issy will act as a distraction for playboy Gianni—then take down his company! But her attraction to him is as intense as it is unexpected... Soon, Issy's charade leads to very real vows!

After working undercover for two years at Rossi Industries, Amelia can't wait any longer for vengeance. Until she spends one incendiary night of passion with Alessandro—which has consequences! Now that she's pregnant with his child, will revenge still be what Amelia wants?

Read Issy and Gianni's story
Bound by the Italian's "I Do"
by Michelle Smart

Discover Amelia and Alessandro's story
Expecting Her Enemy's Heir
by Pippa Roscoe

Both available now!

Pippa Roscoe

EXPECTING HER ENEMY'S HEIR

HARLEQUIN®
PRESENTS™

Recycling programs
for this product may
not exist in your area.

ISBN-13: 978-1-335-73927-8

Expecting Her Enemy's Heir

Copyright © 2023 by Pippa Roscoe

For questions and comments about the quality of this book, please contact us at CustomerService@Harlequin.com.

Harlequin Enterprises ULC
22 Adelaide St. West, 41st Floor
Toronto, Ontario M5H 4E3, Canada
www.Harlequin.com

Printed in U.S.A.

Pippa Roscoe lives in Norfolk near her family and makes daily promises to herself that this is the day she'll leave the computer to take a long walk in the countryside. She can't remember a time when she wasn't dreaming about handsome heroes and innocent heroines. Totally her mother's fault, of course—she gave Pippa her first romance to read at the age of seven! She is inconceivably happy that she gets to share those daydreams with you all. Follow her on Twitter, @pipparoscoe.

Books by Pippa Roscoe

Harlequin Presents

The Wife the Spaniard Never Forgot

The Diamond Inheritance

Terms of Their Costa Rican Temptation
From One Night to Desert Queen
The Greek Secret She Carries

The Royals of Svardia

Snowbound with His Forbidden Princess
Stolen from Her Royal Wedding
Claimed to Save His Crown

Visit the Author Profile page
at Harlequin.com for more titles.

For Michelle,

Who knew exactly what I meant when I said,
"and he kept the land because..."

Working with people that understand you is a
dream but being friends with them is a gift.

Loves ya!

CHAPTER ONE

TODAY WAS THE DAY.

Amelia Seymore peered through the window at the dark grey clouds on the horizon, while early morning joggers and cyclists risked life and limb in the narrow juncture between the bus and the pavement. The start, stop of the number 176 as it crawled north across the bridge was making her nauseous, but it was the smell of damp wool and deodorant that forced her from the bus a stop early, gasping for fresh air. Or at least as fresh as you got in Central London during peak commuter hours. Amelia shook her head trying to regain the focus and sense of stability she had a reputation for. Maybe she was coming down with something.

Get yourself together, she ordered herself firmly. Nothing could distract her or knock her off course. Today had been ten years in the making, but it wasn't the long hours, sleepless nights or the punishingly hard work that steeled her. It was the memory of her father's face the last time they had spoken. The look in his eyes as he had turned away from her, his shaking hand reaching for the bottle of whisky on his desk. *That* was the reason she and her sister, Issy, were doing this. That was why she *had* to succeed today.

Scanning the four-lane road, and too impatient to wait at the lights, Amelia skipped behind a cyclist and in front of a police car. Waving an awkward 'oops' at the cops, she arrived in front of a building considered to be the brightest addition to the crown jewels of the London skyline. While the Shard glittered like a diamond and the Gherkin shone emerald green, the imposing rose-hued building that housed Rossi Industries had been affectionately nicknamed The Ruby and was considered the perfect edifice for the two devastatingly handsome property tycoons who owned it.

Amelia craned her neck to look up at the impressive head office of the international conglomerate that inspired both awe and anger in her. Every single day for the last two years she had made this same walk, knowing that she was entering the lair of the two men that had destroyed her family. And every single day she had promised herself and her sister that they would have their revenge.

Vengeance hadn't come naturally to Amelia. And it certainly hadn't been immediate. She and her sister had been fifteen and thirteen, respectively, when they had first seen Alessandro and Gianni Rossi. Not that they'd known who they were back then. No, they had simply been two young men who had interrupted a Sunday roast to speak with their father. And in one conversation, the Rossi cousins had stolen their father's company out from under him and decimated everything that she and her sister had ever known.

Cold fury tripped down her spine as she retrieved the ID swipe card that proclaimed her Project Manager for Rossi Industries and entered the building. Amelia smiled at the security guard in spite of the memories that held her stomach in a vice, passing through the barriers to the bank of lifts that would take her to the sixty-fourth floor.

As she waited in the deserted lobby for the lift to arrive, she counted down the floors as if it were a ticking bomb the Rossis had no idea of and she *relished* that today would be the day their world shattered, just as hers and Issy's had. And then it wouldn't matter if she had nearly thrown it all away in one night, just over a month ago…

We shouldn't be doing this.

Amelia clenched her teeth, trying to ignore the way the rough, gravelly voice rubbed against her skin even now and once again desire wrapped around a part of her she'd never known she had. A desire that hit her like a tsunami, drawing her beneath the surface and snaring her in the undertow.

I… I want to.

With those three words she had betrayed her family, her sister, *herself.*

No!

She wouldn't let that one night, that one *mistake*, ruin

everything she and Issy had worked so hard for. Yes, she had spent one illicit night with her boss—her enemy— Alessandro Rossi. But it didn't change anything. She just had to ignore the cascade of erotic memories that haunted her. Because no matter what had happened six weeks ago in Hong Kong, it in no way justified or excused what Alessandro and Gianni had done ten years ago to her family. And because of that, today was the day that the Rossi cousins would fall.

Alessandro looked out of the floor-to-ceiling window of his penthouse office to see London stretched out below him like a supplicant. Power. It ran through his veins, not just because of his immeasurable wealth, or the considerable achievements he and his cousin had accomplished in the years since they claimed control of their first business. It might have once belonged to another, but it had flourished into an empire under the Rossi name. No, the power came from the knowledge that the first meeting of his very busy day would green light a deal that promised to send shock waves through the business world.

The Rossi name was already renowned, but this deal would see it written in the history books. In years to come, there might even be two young upstarts who would read of the Rossi name and success and think— *that's what I want to be.*

Alessandro caught the grim smile on the face of his reflection and nodded. How would his father feel when he saw it? When he heard that Alessandro and Gianni had achieved success beyond his wildest dreams…but not under the name of the men who had fathered them. *No.* The first chance he and Gianni got, they legally changed their names, desperate to erase the stain of their fathers in a way that they would feel to the core of their blackened souls. They had chosen Rossi to honour their *nonna*—the only member of their family who had truly shown them kindness.

My blood runs in your veins, boy. And it will run in your children's and your children's children's.

But his father's warning was irrelevant. The blood line would end with him. He would make sure of it.

Not that Alessandro indulged in self-sabotage. Rossi Industries was his life, consuming all his time and energy. Where his father sought to destroy and strangle the last breath from the vineyards he overworked, or the wife he had constantly abused, Alessandro was determined to leave the world better than it had been; *that* was his legacy.

His watch beeped with a fifteen-minute alert for the morning's meeting. It really was bad timing that it coincided with Gianni's one and utterly immoveable holiday of the year. But, he reminded himself, the Aurora deal had been vetted by his cousin, everyone on the board, by his most trusted advisors, and the project manager he trusted far more quickly than was deserved after just two years of service.

Amelia Seymore.

Alessandro straightened the knot in his tie, check-ing the button behind it, but in his mind he was undo-ing the button and yanking the tie from his neck as he watched that same woman looking at him, breathless want filling her words.

I... I want you.

Are you sure, Amelia? Because—

Just tonight. Just now. But we will never speak of it. Ever.

He'd been so desperate for another taste of her lips he'd have agreed to anything. *Cristo*, if she'd known how much power she'd wielded in that moment, she could have had him on his knees begging to give her everything he owned. Embarrassment crept up his neck in angry red patches.

He flexed his hand, the memory of her naked thigh beneath his palm taunting him, leading him deeper into the one night—the *only* night—he'd crossed a line both professionally and personally. A line that was as much a taboo as it was utterly wrong. Shame, thick, heavy and ugly, crawled across his skin. He wasn't *that man*—he didn't sleep with his staff. Only apparently he was.

We will never speak of it.

A knock cut through the memory of Amelia's edict and he returned to the seat behind his desk, hiding the near constant state of arousal he'd been in since he and Amelia Seymore had returned from the successful deal in Hong Kong six weeks ago.

'Come.'

His secretary entered the room two strides and stopped, having learned quickly that he liked his space.

'There are no changes to the schedule for today. Asimov has checked into his hotel and he and his people will be here for the eleven a.m. briefing. Lunch is booked at Alain Ducasse at The Dorchester and Gianni called to say, "Don't mess it up."'

'He said "mess"?' Alessandro queried.

'I'm paraphrasing.'

Alessandro held back the smirk at what his cousin would have really said. Raised as close as brothers, their knowledge of each other's thoughts was only one of the reasons for their immense success.

'And the nine a.m. meeting?' he asked his secretary.

'The room is set up, the audio and visuals have been tested by IT, Ms Seymore is already in the room and has given me a spare presentation pack for you to view now, if you'd like.'

'That won't be necessary.'

And it really wouldn't. If Amelia Seymore said that she'd do something, she did it. She assessed projects, met with clients, ran projections, assessed workflows and got it done. She was nearly as exacting as himself. Which was why he'd entrusted the Aurora project to her. Not because they had shared one utterly incendiary and completely forbidden night together, but because she was excellent at her job, always early, always correct and always had the right answer. She could have been made purposefully for him.

'Sir?'

If only she didn't distract him in ways that no other person had ever done.

'Repeat the question?' he forced himself to ask, as distasteful as he found it.

'Would you like your coffee in here, or down at the meeting?'

'Here.' Clearly, he needed to gather himself.

As members of her team filtered into the glass-walled meeting room, Amelia lined up the presentation packs with the notebooks and pens she'd asked Housekeeping to provide. Alessandro was particular, he liked things neat and exact.

And he'd liked the way she'd sounded when—

Red slashes heated her cheeks and a light sweat broke out across her shoulders. She slammed the door shut on her memories, trying to ground herself in the moment. Stepping back from the large boardroom table, she caught sight of the sketch of the building that might have changed the face of inner-city apartment living across the world, had the Rossi cousins not built their empire on the back of her father's broken soul. Really, Alessandro and Gianni had brought this on themselves.

For ten years *this* was what she and Issy had planned for. The stars had aligned in a way that had seemed almost preordained. After two years of project after project, Amelia's position within RI was unquestionable. And because of that, the most important project the

Rossis had ever undertaken was in her hands, just as Gianni's annual holiday broached the horizon. Everyone knew that together Alessandro and Gianni were undefeatable. But separated? It was the only time there was a chink in their legendary armour. A chink that Amelia and her sister would use to bring them to their knees.

Issy had spent years turning herself into the perfect distraction for the legendary playboy with his own hashtag #TheHotRossi. Yesterday, an Issy styled perfectly to Gianni's tastes had flown to the Caribbean with the sole purpose of luring him onto a boat and keeping him away from Alessandro while the final decision on Aurora deal was made. And with Gianni safely out of contact, Amelia could now commit the greatest act of industrial sabotage ever recorded, ensuring that the Rossis' world was left as obliterated as hers and her sister's had been.

We're doing the right thing, aren't we?

The question Issy had asked before she left for the airport yesterday had poked and prodded at Amelia's conscience. Not because Amelia didn't absolutely know that they were doing the right thing, because she *did*. But in order to set their plan in motion, she had been forced to lie to her sister. Something she'd never thought she'd ever do.

Years before, when they had first started their quest for vengeance, they had made a pact. *No revenge without proof of corruption.* From even the beginning they had refused to become the very monsters they hunted.

And, of course, Amelia had agreed. Because there *would* be a paper trail. There *would* be evidence of countless corrupt deals and ruined businesses Alessandro and Gianni had left in their wake on their journey to becoming a globally recognised name in property development. But in two years she'd found...*nothing*. Nothing other than what had been done to their father.

Panic had begun to nip at her heels. What if she could never give Issy the justice she'd promised her? What if everything they'd sacrificed to achieve their revenge was for nothing? While normal teenage girls had been going to parties and clubs, Issy and Amelia Seymore had planned and plotted. Amelia had forced herself through every business course and language module possible to make herself the perfect future employee for Rossi Industries. And her sister? Issy had trawled through the online world, researching every inch of their enemies' lives. No corporate press release, business deal, tweet or social media post was left unseen. They had spent *years* on their mission, forsaking so much of their teenage and young adult years.

But then had come the business trip to Hong Kong; her third major project with Rossi Industries and one she and her team had invested months of work on. Alessandro wasn't supposed to have flown out for the meeting himself. It was highly unusual, but she hadn't let it put her off her stride. She'd nailed the presentation, and the strong relationship she'd built with the client had earned them not only the commission but a personal invitation for her and Alessandro to dine with Kai Choi. It would have been a grave insult to refuse, so while her team members had returned to London, she and Alessandro had remained in Hong Kong.

Even now she was shocked by how thrilled she'd been to land the deal. Amelia's job was supposed to be a ruse. A means to an end. But instead, the dizzying excitement she'd felt had been reflected in the eyes of the very man whose opinion should matter least. Eyes that had turned excitement into heat after holding her gaze for just a little too long. Her heart jerked in her chest, as if it were tied to the memory of the moment that the line between them had been shattered.

A shattering that had forced her to do something she had never intended. She couldn't wait to find proof any more. The guilt, tension, the *desire* she still felt for a man who had destroyed her family was pulling her apart from the inside, spinning her further away from the control that she was known for. Amelia's plans were beginning to unravel, her command of the situation slipping from her fingers like sand.

So, she had done the unthinkable.

Amelia had told her sister that she'd found proof of their corruption and, in doing so, set in motion the takedown of the Rossi cousins. It was a lie that would take Issy's trust—the beautiful, delicate but utterly unbreakable thing that it was—and break it. Amelia had betrayed the one person who had been her constant companion since the death of their father and the emotional and physical retreat of their mother. Issy, who was bright and lovely and always, unfailingly, *good*. Just the thought of it chipped away at the crack that had formed in her heart, even as she told herself that she had done it for the right reason. The Rossis *needed* punishing.

Thomas Seymore had died by their hands as surely as if they'd killed him themselves. The demons sent by Alessandro and Gianni had haunted their father until he had finally drunk himself into an early grave—never recovering from the damage done to his reputation or status. And their mother? She had never been the same. Leaving their friends, their school, their social circle, losing her husband, declaring bankruptcy had broken something in the once vibrant Jane Seymore and no matter what Amelia and Issy had done, their mother had never come back to them.

'I hope Gianni comes back soon. I hate meetings when it's just Alessandro.'

'He's such a ballbreaker.'

'At least by the end of this meeting we'll know which company the project will partner with. The back and forth has been going on for months.'

For the first time that morning, the erratic beat of Amelia's heart settled because this was it. At the end of this meeting, she would guide Rossi Industries to partner with the wrong company and seal their fate. She would deliver Issy the revenge that Amelia had promised her ten years before and finally, *finally*, they would be done with this; she would walk away and never look back.

The room went quiet and she looked up to see Alessandro take his seat at the head of the table. When everyone was sitting up, backs straight, silent and waiting, he nodded for Amelia to begin what would be the last deal Rossi Industries ever undertook.

Today was the day.

Alessandro turned a page on the printout Amelia had provided the team. She was articulate and concise—nothing was wasted. Even the image she presented was considered; elegant but subtle, nothing intrusive, almost nothing memorable. He imagined she'd rehearsed the presentation over and over again. He would have, in her position. She stood to the left of the large screen displaying the two companies vying for partnership on this once-in-a-lifetime opportunity, the gentle glow of the screen making her nothing more than a silhouette.

Just as she had been against the gauzy curtain of the hotel room in Hong Kong when he'd reached for the tie holding her wrap dress together and pulled. The dress had sighed open to reveal perfection. The black-lace-underwear-embellished skin that drew his hand like a magnet. The slide of his palm over the smooth planes set off a wave of restlessness that crested over her body, her breasts heaving with each inhalation and when he reached for her, his own body trembled.

'And this is the problem we have,' Amelia claimed

to the room, bringing him back to the present with a
start he managed to disguise by reaching for his coffee,
when caffeine was patently the last thing he needed.

He tuned out her words, remembering the first time
he'd encountered her. His attention had snagged on her
name, linking her to a moment in time that Alessandro
refused to dwell on. Her file had revealed an impressive academic record, a notable drive, and enthusiastic
references. She had interviewed well and he was sure
that she would excel in her role, just like all of RI's
other employees. And it should have ended there. But…

She had ignored him.

And that was unusual. It wasn't arrogance talking, but experience. Over the years, Alessandro had
attracted as much attention as his charming playboy
cousin, Gianni. He simply chose not to indulge. Alessandro had no desire to entertain anyone with expecta-
tions of a *more* he had absolutely no interest in pursuing.
Which had earned him the nickname 'The Monk'. Despite this, it hadn't escaped Alessandro's notice that the
looks he owed to an impressive combination of genes
attracted a certain amount of attention, wanted or not.
Yet, Amelia Seymore had treated him with the same
cool impartiality as she did every other colleague in the
building. It might not have made her close friends with
her colleagues, but her talent and efficiency were undeniable, and she impressed her managers and team alike.

Her hair—rich admittedly, with reds and chestnuts
and hints of golds—was always up, efficient in a bun,

or plait, or some kind of twist that Alessandro was sure defied the laws of gravity. He shouldn't know that when it was down, it reached just below her shoulder blades, curled with the curve of her breast and curtained over nipples that were a fascinating shade of pink.

Her features were small, equally proportioned to ensure that nothing stood out, except that they *all* stood out. Lips of the palest pink that were neither lush, nor dramatically shaped into a bow, but that had explored his body with a ravenous fascination that had driven him to the edge of his control. The arch of a mahogany eyebrow framed her face in perfect symmetry with the line of a jaw that had fitted perfectly in the palm of his hand, concealing a pulse point behind her ear that flushed when she became aroused.

An arousal that when he had lain between her thighs, her body trembling beneath his touch, the wet heat welcoming him, calling to him, enticing him to taste, to tease, to—

Cristo.

He cleared his throat and the entire boardroom looked up at him. Amelia pinned him with a gaze that showed nothing but professionalism—and yet he still felt her censure. A flick of his hand and she continued.

'It is clear that this decision is one of utmost importance and will shape the face of not only the project, but the future of this company.'

He needed better control over himself. Control that Amelia seemed to have mastered.

She had been true to her word. Absolutely nothing had changed. It was almost as if it had never happened. Which was absolutely for the best, he assured himself. Once this meeting was done, and the choice of partnership had been decided, he would have nothing further to do with Amelia Seymore other than as a name on paperwork pertaining to the project. There would be no need for any kind of interaction other than that, which, Alessandro decided firmly, was most definitely a good thing.

As Amelia began wrapping up the presentation, a sense of eager expectation filled the room. Her team wanted to get this decision made and move on, but they had no idea of the true consequences that would follow which company was chosen.

Everything about the presentation had been created to seem as if she was offering them a choice between Chapel Developments and Firstview Ltd. If Rossi Industries partnered with Chapel Developments, then it would be the most successful partnership in the property development world working on a venture that was as daring as it was creatively ingenious. But if they chose to partner with Firstview Ltd, then every hope and dream in this room would turn into a nightmare. Firstview didn't have the infrastructure or the financial backing to support the project to fruition. Of course, Amelia had worked incredibly hard to ensure that wasn't evident in the least, but a partnership would be the ruin of them all.

She looked at Alessandro's leadership team—she could see it in their eyes. Respect, understanding, eagerness and more than just a little avarice. This deal could make them billionaires in their own right. And it turned her stomach. Greed, the same greed that had destroyed her family. The nausea hit her hard again, throwing her momentarily. As if needing to see the one person her vengeance hung on, she looked up to find Alessandro's gaze firmly on hers. Waves of unnatural fire arced across her body, short-circuiting her brain for just a nanosecond—and she remembered. Remembered the crushing endlessness of the orgasm he had given her, flooding her body with a rush she'd never experienced, one that had threatened to undo everything she'd known, everything she'd sacrificed. And in the crushing aftermath of that wave, she found her voice.

'My suggestion is that Firstview is the only possible way forward to achieve the desired outcome.'

And with that one sentence, she started the process of destroying one of the biggest property companies in the world—ensuring that finally, ten years after Alessandro and Gianni had taken everything from Amelia and her sister, they would know how it felt for their world to crumble.

CHAPTER TWO

SOMETHING WAS WRONG, but Alessandro couldn't put his finger on what. The feeling had started around the time that Amelia wrapped up her presentation that morning, successfully getting one hundred per cent agreement on her partnership proposal for the Aurora project.

He checked his watch. The day had all but disappeared. If he left now, he might be able to make it back in time to hit the gym, grab dinner and check over the Aurora contracts for whatever it was his subconscious was snagging on. In the ten years since he and Gianni had taken the Englishman's business and turned it into an empire, Alessandro had learned to trust his gut. And his gut was telling him that something was wrong.

Alessandro was tempted to call Gianni. He'd messaged him earlier about the decision to move ahead with Firstview Ltd, but his cousin's yearly holiday was sacrosanct and Alessandro disliked the idea of disrupting it. Outside the twelve days Gianni spent each year in the Caribbean, he worked as if the Devil himself held the reins and he deserved the break. Alessandro switched off his computer, grabbed his jacket, turned off the lights in his office and made his way towards the elevator that ran through the centre of the building.

Designed by Rob Weller, the Rossis' preferred architect, the atrium that extended through the entire building was a marvel. Built five years ago, Rossi Industries rented out the lower floors to various businesses, a newspaper and a TV studio. But the upper levels were used solely by RI and had been created with meticulous eye for detail and consideration for the needs and well-being of his staff.

The dynamic open-plan design made the most of the natural light brought into the building through lightly tinted windows. Rose on the outside but not on the inside, the light worked with the white accents to create a bright, easy space in which to be. Social spaces were balanced with work areas, with healthcare facilities, staff restaurant, a gym, and a landscaped terrace and café on the wraparound balcony. The roof garden was accessible by only his and Gianni's offices on the penthouse floor, but was often used as a space for company events.

Alessandro was proud of what they had achieved. Pleased to know that Rossi Industries was a company that looked after its staff, never wanting them to push themselves to the brink, always knowing that the health of his staff was first and foremost to him.

I don't care how tired you are. There is more work to be done.

Refusing to shy away from the vicious childhood memory of his father's demands, Alessandro embraced it. Happy to know that he had walked away from his childhood refusing to be cowed by the mean-spirited, violent man. Everything he'd done was to ensure that he was nothing like Saverio Vizzini.

When the lift arrived, he faced the 'back', which displayed all the floors and staff areas of Rossi Industries. With the evening pouring into the building, the few lights bouncing off glass meeting rooms and breakout areas sparkled like stars in the night sky. Housekeeping staff would turn off any forgotten lights but one in particular caught his eye, and he'd pressed the corresponding floor's button before he knew it.

For one brief moment he wavered. Told himself not to get out of the lift. To continue on to the parking level and leave. He wondered, later, what might have happened if he had. Whether things would have been different and whether he'd have wanted them to be. In the end it didn't much matter. Things had been set in motion long before that day, and Alessandro doubted that he'd have managed to escape them.

They'd done it. Amelia had sent Issy a message to let her know that Rossi Industries had taken the bait, that Alessandro's and Gianni's destruction was all but assured. Not that the end of Alessandro and Gianni would be immediate. No, her plan of vengeance hadn't been as simple as a swift, painless death.

Just like what had happened to her father, to her mother and the lives she and her sister had known, the destruction of Rossi Industries would take months, perhaps even as long as a year if Firstview managed to hide their ineptitude better than she thought they might. But Amelia would be long gone by then. She would be offered 'a job that she couldn't refuse' and she would leave, without even seeing out her notice. There was, of course, no dream job. Amelia Seymore would simply disappear into thin air.

All she needed to do now was wait out the next few days while the contracts with Firstview Ltd were signed, then Issy could leave Gianni in the Caribbean and return to the UK and the sisters could celebrate.

But Amelia didn't feel like celebrating. Instead she was effectively emptying her desk. Not so that anyone would notice, because she'd need to continue to work here for the next few days, she rationalised. But when the time came, it would probably be best if she was able to make a quick exit. A *very* quick exit.

He would be so angry.

It didn't matter, she told herself firmly, resenting the way that even a small part of her worried about Alessandro. Guilt throbbed in her heart, knowing that her immediate concern should be her sister, not a man who had caused such irreparable damage to her family.

She had just switched her computer off when the hairs on the back of her neck lifted and her heart beat a little too late and a little too hard. *He* was there. She didn't have to turn around to look. She *knew* it. Unbidden, his words from that night ran through her mind like raindrops.

If this is only for one night, then I would give you everything you could ever want for. You only need to ask. So ask me, cara. *Ask, and I will make it so.*

She'd asked for things she'd never even dreamed of in a moment of unbridled desperate desire and he'd done them and more.

'Amelia?'

She couldn't face him, not yet. Not when she had to bite her lip to stop herself from crying out in need, in want. Instead, she did the only thing she was capable of and nodded. Inexplicably, her eyes felt damp.

Was she crying? For *him* or for herself?

Enough!

She pasted a bright smile on her face and turned to meet him.

'Mr Rossi. What can I do for you?'

Something flashed in his eyes, hot, angry even, but it was gone in less than one of her frantic heartbeats. She thought she saw him look to her neck—where he had pressed open-mouthed kisses before drowning her in a pleasure she never knew existed, before he had taken possession of her body and—

'What are you still doing here?' Alessandro asked.

'Just finishing a few things. I was just…leaving,' she said, realising that he was too. Now she was going to be stuck in a lift with him for the entire journey down to

the ground floor. 'You?' she asked, inanely because…
well. What really was there to say to a man she had
slept with and was on the brink of completely and utterly destroying?

'On my way out,' he replied, his features almost too
guarded, as if he knew exactly how silly this conversation was.

Neither of them moved. Instead, the silence spun a
cocoon around them, the air thickened by heated looks
and unsteady breaths. Her desire pawed at her when
she noticed his hand flex by his thigh. A hand that had
caressed her skin, had delved between her legs, had
pulled her harder and deeper against his open mouth.

Could he hear the thud of her heart? The way that her
breath caught in her throat? His gaze flickered between
her lips and her eyes before he turned away, her heart
aching and angry and wanting and she didn't know any
more. If only he weren't so *handsome*.

His body was angled proprietorially towards her and
she felt crowded even though there were nearly two feet
between them. The powerful cords of his neck stood
out as he reached up to fuss with his tie knot, the deep
tan of his skin rich and evocative next to the starched
white origami-like fold of his collar. A stubble Amelia
was half convinced that he hated was already visible
across his jawline and neck, and she was haunted by
the memory of how it had felt beneath her fingertips,
how it had sounded as she'd explored every single inch
of him that night.

The broad shoulders she'd gripped, the lush thick raven-dark hair she'd fisted in her hands as he'd thrust into her. Amelia hated to think that she had been brought so low by good looks, but what else could it have been? The man had utterly destroyed her family and she had all but begged him to ruin her too as she had gripped the edge of the table in his hotel suite. She'd spread her legs wider, to make room for him between them, her body welcoming the hard angles of his hips. The brush of his arousal at her core had sent a gasp through her body…

Amelia slammed the door shut on a memory she should have buried so deep she could never find it again. The only way she'd survived the last six weeks was knowing that they'd never speak of what had happened in Hong Kong. Keeping it tucked away behind a pane of impenetrable glass was the only thing that had kept her sane.

'Shall we?' she asked, assuming the emotionally indifferent tone she had worn for two years, as if she didn't feel torn apart by the weight of desire and the need for a vengeance that had begun to taste bitter in the last few months.

Amelia's breezy tone ate at Alessandro. There he was feeling as if his life had been upended by this innocuous English girl, and she was utterly unaffected by the most sensuous night of his life. Perhaps somewhere in the recent years of his *'Monkdom'*, he had developed perversions. The thought horrified him so much that for a shocking moment, he stilled, causing a flash of concern to pass across Amelia's features.

'Are you—?'

He turned on his heel and stalked back towards the lifts. He should never have stopped on her floor. Once again he wrestled with that sense of frustrated desire and shame. Resisting the urge to pull at his collar, he reminded himself that he had taken advantage of a junior member of staff and he deserved every ounce of inner turmoil that he was currently struggling with.

Crossing the floor, he recognised that it had been rude to cut her off mid-sentence but had he not, he might have—*God forbid*—actually answered her question and admitted that no, he wasn't okay in the slightest and was, in fact, being driven out of his mind with a need for her that felt unnatural.

'Maybe I should take the stairs,' he said as they reached the lift, realising that he probably shouldn't be taking the lift with her.

A slight frown across her brow appeared to question the sense in walking down *sixty-four* flights of stairs. And now he couldn't ignore the fact that he'd just volunteered to do precisely that in order to avoid spending the minute and a half journey with her in the lift.

She blinked at him, shutters over an unfathomable gaze, and turned to face the elevator doors. 'If you like,' she said.

Her response had him grinding his teeth and he was about to leave when the lift arrived, the doors sliding open, and now there was no escape. Leaving would be the height of stupidity, showing the exact extent of how much her presence affected him *beyond* what he had already revealed.

He gestured for her to enter before him and he caught her glancing at his hand before she stepped into the lift. As she turned to look out into the centre of the building he saw the delicate blush at the pulse point behind her ear, his gaze snagging on the way her shirt had come open beneath the pull of the strap of her bag on her shoulder.

Heat crawled across his shoulders, making Alessandro want to yank at the collar of his shirt. She wasn't as unaffected as she appeared and just the thought of that enflamed *everything*. This time, instead of staying in the lift he should damn well get out. Alessandro closed his eyes but instead of blessed darkness he saw her straddled across his lap, taking him deep within her, riding a sensuous wave that consumed them both. The doors closed behind him and the lurch in his gut had nothing to do with the gentle descent.

'Congratulations,' he forced out through numb lips.

For a moment, he thought he saw guilt flash in the golden green depths of eyes that he had once, inconceivably, thought unnoteworthy. But he must have been projecting, because the guilt was his burden to bear.

'Thank you,' Amelia said before biting her lip and turning her attention back to the floors flying past the glass windows.

'Are you celebrating?' he asked.

Minchione! Clearly, she didn't want to speak to him and no wonder. The burning shame of self-loathing now heated his internal body temperature rather than arousal and he was unusually thankful for it.

'No, my sister is…'

Amelia swallowed her words, wishing she could have bitten off her own tongue. 'Away,' she concluded, aware that Alessandro was waiting for her to finish her sentence. Oh, God, this was her punishment. To be stuck in a small enclosed space with the man she'd just ruined— the man that, in spite of everything, she still wanted with a desperation that left her breathless.

Enemy, enemy, enemy!

'What was that?' Alessandro asked, bending slightly as if to listen more closely.

Instinctively she jerked away from him and instantly regretted it. From the tic in his jaw, Alessandro hadn't missed it. His hands fisted by his thighs and oh, God, what was wrong with her? Why was that so sexy?

She had become a stranger to herself in the last six weeks. Ever since she had secured the deal in Hong Kong, something had changed. Because how could she recognise the woman who would sleep with the man that destroyed her family? How could she have betrayed everything she and her sister had worked towards? How could she have weighed one night of pleasure with a childhood of misery and chosen *him*?

Once again a wetness pressed against the backs of

her eyes. Not here. And not now! She just needed to get out of this lift and away from Alessandro Rossi. She could have her breakdown when she was home.

Count to ten, darling, and it will be fine.

But the words she'd whispered to her sister through their teenage years didn't work this time. It wouldn't be fine. Issy was off in the Caribbean somewhere, having kidnapped Gianni Rossi, and she was lusting after a man who was the Devil incarnate.

She hadn't expected it to feel like this. Wasn't she supposed to feel victorious? Wasn't it supposed to be amazing, this feeling? Vengeance almost guaranteed, it should have been the crowning achievement of all she'd ever wanted. But she didn't. Instead she felt…*guilty.* She felt sick. And shivery. And no, she hadn't come down with a cold. But…something was *wrong.*

'If this is…' he said, and trailed off, awkwardness looking strange on Alessandro's handsome features. She'd never seen him like this. In the boardroom he was powerful, determined…confidence didn't even factor, it was something beyond that. A supreme self-belief. And the night they'd shared in Hong Kong? A shiver ran the length of her spine. He'd unlocked fantasies that night she'd never even known she'd had. 'If you want to speak to HR… I think we should speak to HR.'

Her head snapped up out of the desire-dazed fog. She almost laughed. She *wanted* to, absurdly. In three days' time, their one night in Hong Kong would be the least of his problems. She would be gone and Alessandro Rossi would never see her again, no matter how hard he might look.

'I don't know what you think we would need to speak to HR about,' she said, purposefully keeping her face blank.

He frowned, his eyes, usually so clear, clouded and confused, she almost didn't like to see it.

'Hong Kong,' he said, as if trying to find a tether to hold onto in the conversation that was clearly difficult.

'Hong Kong was a roaring success. We finalised the deal with Kai Choi, went for dinner with him and his team to celebrate, and then I returned to my hotel room and you returned to yours. I'm not exactly sure why we would need to share that with HR.'

'So, nothing happened?'

'Nothing happened.' It couldn't have. Because she couldn't have been that person. Shame and guilt—and the traces of a desire so heavy it still ran in her veins—made her just a little dizzy.

Alessandro nearly reached out a hand to Amelia as she swayed a little. But she flickered an angry gaze at where his hand twitched and he stopped himself just in time.

Because, of course, grabbing her right now, putting his hands on her was an excellent *idea.*

Alessandro was really beginning to dislike his inner voice, though he could hardly argue with being called a fool. He opened his mouth to object to Amelia's statement. Because there was something inherently wrong about her denying that night had happened. Denying that what they'd shared had happened. Because it had.

Unlike Gianni, Alessandro stayed out of the limelight. His photograph was never in the newspapers, his name only appearing in print if linked to his cousin. He was not instantly recognisable to the person on the street, and were they ever asked if they knew of him, their answer would be 'Alessandro who?' His privacy was a closely guarded thing, so Alessandro could perhaps forgive Amelia for thinking that he did this kind of thing all the time. Not with staff—no, she had at least, thankfully, acknowledged that it was unusual for both of them.

But beyond that, the last time he had shared a bed with someone had been… He tried to think back. Years? Certainly more than two. He was incredibly discerning in his choice of partners, in what attracted him, which was why he had been so shocked to find that Amelia, the perfect employee, who on the surface could have defined English 'plainness', had grabbed his attention and yanked on it, leading him into a night that had proved as unforgettable as it was indescribable.

So he was about to reply, to refute her statement, to tell her that he knew it wasn't just him affected by that night, that he wanted more, to tell her all of the most asinine things that it had never once occurred to him to say to another human being before now, when the doors to the lift opened and Amelia practically ran out into the foyer.

'Amelia,' he called after her as she hurried towards the exit, no longer caring who saw or heard him.

'See you tomorrow, Mr Rossi,' she called over her shoulder without looking back.

He stood, in the centre of the atrium, watching her leave through the main entrance to The Ruby and thought, *yes*. He *would* see her tomorrow. And this time, he'd not let her run away, because he hadn't missed the way that her breath had caught, that her pulse had flickered, and her skin had crested pink with desire. It wasn't just him in this madness. It couldn't be.

He was brought back to earth by a ringtone reserved exclusively for his cousin and could only imagine what Gianni would say when he confessed his sin of sleeping with a junior member of staff. Their lawyers would have a field day.

'Gianni, how—?'

'Andro, listen, I don't have much time.'

'Okay, but what's the—?'

'Amelia Seymore,' Gianni interrupted. 'She's Thomas Seymore's daughter.'

'What?' Alessandro demanded. 'I can't hear you properly.' He *couldn't* have heard Gianni properly. It was just the crackle on the line.

'Listen to me, Amelia Seymore is a traitor. She's been…spy this whole time. She's…with her sister to destroy us.'

'Amelia Seymore?' Alessandro repeated like an idiot,

the line was so bad, but he knew if he wanted to he could read between the crackle.

'Yes! Seymore. The…project is compromised.'

'Which project?' he demanded, but he realised Gianni hadn't heard his question.

'And listen, she claims to have found some kind of proof of corruption against us.'

'Corruption? What corruption?' The line was getting even worse. Frustration and incredulity were vying to escape the tight fist he had on his emotions.

'I don't know, but…the messages I read, Amelia… found evidence of corruption… I'm in the Caribbean with her sister. I'll…and stop her communicating with anyone and causing any more damage. Can you deal with Amelia? This needs to be nipped in the bud and damage limitation undertaken immediately.'

'Consider it done,' Alessandro growled darkly.

'I maybe out of reach for a while, but I'll try and get a message to you when I know what's going on.'

'Likewise. Speak soon, cousin.'

When Alessandro ended the call, his jaw was clenched so tight it had started to ache. He was *still* standing in the centre of the atrium, *still* looking at where he had last seen Amelia.

She was Thomas Seymore's daughter, come to destroy them?

He scoffed, surely not. Amelia? Capable of sabotage? No. The thought was so strong that he gestured with his hand, cutting through the empty air. But then a montage flickered through his mind. Amelia hesitant, guilty, conflicted, angry…

My sister is away…

And suddenly it all started to make sense. Fury found its way into his veins and travelled throughout his body in a single pump of his heart. *Cristo*, he could have laughed at himself. He'd been so stupid. Taken in by the oldest of ruses. He shook his head in disgust. And he'd more than simply let her. He'd asked her for it, *begged* her to let him sign his own ruination. But it wasn't just his own—it was his cousin's, it was his company, his staff…

No!

Gianni had warned him in time. Alessandro still had a chance to turn things around. He spun on his heel and, instead of going home to his apartment, he went back up to his office and started to plan. Thomas Seymore's daughters had no idea what they had started and he and Gianni would make damn sure they would live to regret the day they messed with the Rossi cousins.

CHAPTER THREE

HANDS BRACED AGAINST the sink, Amelia stared at herself in the mirror the next morning. Accusations and sleeplessness had drawn dark slashes beneath her eyes and she looked unnaturally pale, even considering the harsh bathroom lighting.

You can do this, she told herself sternly. *It's two measly days. Alessandro will be in meetings for most, if not all, of that time.* All she had to do was play nice with her team for two days. All she had to do was smile.

All she had to do was let go of the sink.

She released the death grip she'd had on the porcelain and with one last glare at herself in the mirror, she grabbed her jacket and bag and let herself out of the small flat she shared with her sister in Brockley. The broken lift and the unusual heatwave made the stairwell unbearable and she emerged onto the pavement already hot, sweaty and out of sorts. That was why she came to a stop and simply stared at the sight that met her, genuinely unsure whether it was real or not.

Alessandro was leaning against a sleek black vehicle that to call a car would probably be some kind of insult. Hands fisted deep in his pockets and eyes hidden behind aviator sunglasses that screamed money, he exuded a lazy sexuality that should have come with a health warning. But there was also something else. Something that put her senses on alert.

It was a slow roll of emotion, building to a crescendo as sharp as any sudden fright and she had to press her hand over her heart to keep it in place. She forced herself to take a deep breath, wishing it were still because of the fright, but honestly, the sight of Alessandro made her sex *ache*. A pulse flared across her body, a chain reaction that touched from sense to sense until her whole body practically trembled with want.

'You scared me,' she accused, trying to catch her breath as she searched for a reason why Alessandro Rossi would be waiting on a South London street, for *her*.

Could he know?

No, she dismissed. There was absolutely no way that he could have discovered Firstview's inadequacies already, especially as it had taken her months.

'My sincere apologies, Ms Seymore. I'm afraid we are quite short on time.'

'Time? For what?' Amelia asked, closing the distance between them. There was an unusual tension in the way Alessandro held himself. Dark glasses might have hidden eyes from her, but she sensed that she was under the very intense microscope of his focus.

'We've just received news of an important business proposal and with the Aurora project all wrapped up, you're the only project lead that I can spare.'

Only Alessandro would wrap up one deal the night before and start a new one before coffee the next morning. 'My team needs briefing and there are a few things…' She might not understand what was going on, but, whatever it was, she knew she couldn't spend any more time with him in such close proximity. 'Is there not someone else who could—?'

'I'm afraid not. You are the only person it can be.'

'But—'

'Ms Seymore, is there a problem?' His words were like a leash, yanking her back into place.

'No. Of course not,' she replied as she stepped forward to meet him beside the car. And he still didn't move. Now that she was this close, she could see that he hadn't shaved and the stubble from last night was now a dark swathe across his jaw. A muscle flexed at the hollow just beneath the dark line and she felt the tension thicken between them, building until finally he stepped aside to open the door, gesturing for her to get in.

'Where are we going?' she asked as the car pulled into the road, attracting more than a few stares from neighbours who were understandably shocked to see such an expensive car in the area.

'Not too far.'

He passed her a file, explaining that it was a brief he needed her to read ahead of the meeting. Frowning, she scanned the opening documents outlining a prospective client they were considering. There were nearly fifty pages here and an anxious heat crawled across her shoulders.

Amelia was finding it hard to focus, not just from the motion of the car and trying to read, but the awareness of Alessandro himself. Arm propped up against the window, chin rested in his palm, his gaze glued on some invisible point in the distance.

Concentrate. It was just one meeting and then she'd be back with her team and done for the day before she knew it.

Only, rather than turning off the South Circular into London, they continued to head out east.

'It's a very important deal, Amelia. I'd really like to get it right,' he warned, as if noticing that she was distracted.

'Of course.'

She turned back to the pages and lost herself in what could be an exciting new deal for Rossi Industries. Scanning the projections, the highly sought-after location of the land for sale and the cultural interest in the surrounding area, she could see how it would come together. It would be incredible. Partnering with Chalendar Enterprises was clever and would save Rossi Industries time overall, the two businesses having worked together before.

And even though Amelia wouldn't be there to see it happen, she was already identifying which team members would be best, what areas might be problematic and how to navigate them. In her absence they would probably give the project to Brent Bennet, but he often made mistakes on the contracts. She should give Legal a heads up…only she wouldn't. Because she would be long gone by the time that happened. The car slowed to a stop and she looked out of the window to see tarmac.

'Alessandro, where is this meeting?'

Alessandro said nothing, opening the door of the car and getting out onto the runway of a private airfield just outside London. He said nothing because a worryingly large part of him wanted to shout and rage and yell. But now wasn't the time for that. There was too much at stake.

He held the door to the car open for her and hated the way that, no matter how the shocking discovery of her true identity had blown his world apart, his body hadn't got the memo, and the soft scent of jasmine that rose from her skin as she passed in front of him hardened his arousal as much as his anger.

The betrayal of it. Of her. He would deal with that later, but for now his one focus, his only goal, was to find out what she had done and stop it before the rot could take hold. His plan was simple—isolate, interrogate and eliminate.

No one other than her father, Thomas Seymore, had managed to pull the wool over their eyes so successfully. Alessandro choked back a bitter laugh. He and

Gianni had, naively, believed that they had learned their lesson that one and only time. Clearly, they were mistaken.

And to think she had the gall not to even change her surname. It had been staring him in the face the whole time and what had he done? Smiled at her, thanked her, and asked her for more.

'Sir?'

'*Si?*' he snapped and Lucinda, a member of his air crew who had been with RI for nearly six years, flinched a little. 'My apologies. Truly, Lucinda,' he said, warning himself to keep his cool.

His emotions swung like a giant pendulum, back and forth between the weight of the past and the future of his company.

He watched Amelia settle into a large cream leather seat, fasten the safety belt and look out of the window. She seemed a little disconcerted but he knew, now, just how good an actress she really was.

'Coffee, Mr Rossi?'

'*Grazie mille*, Lucinda,' he replied sincerely, taking the espresso over to a seat on the opposite side of the cabin.

He just needed to get to Villa Vittoria. It might have been a refuge for him and Gianni for the past ten years, but there was also a deep irony in taking Amelia Seymore back to the scene of the crime. He refused to think of it as kidnap, even though his conscience contorted itself in order not to do so. He was simply taking her to a place where he intended to cut her off from any possible forms of communication until he could identify just how badly she had sabotaged his company and the hundreds of thousands of people he employed globally. It was the only solution he had been able to come up with in the twelve hours since he had received the call from Gianni.

When they were safely at the villa, all hell could break loose. He just had to get her there first without her realising what was happening. It was why he'd given her the file, to distract her and keep her from asking too many questions.

'How long has Lexicon been looking to develop the land?' Amelia asked, flicking back and forth between a few pages. Unease gripped his stomach, empty aside from the coffee he'd all but inhaled. He'd not had long to put together the fake file—in half an hour he'd brought together a mishmash of four old, and failed, pitches. But he could play this game better than anyone, he thought, subtly rolling his shoulders. The Seymore sisters had messed with the wrong billionaires.

'A while,' he replied, knowing that she had been seeking a specific answer. A perverse part of him delighted in withholding it, wanting to needle, to irritate, to annoy. It was a small petty victory, but he could not lose sight of the greater picture. Because so much more than his ego depended on him rooting out the damage she had done and putting an end to it immediately.

'We will soon be taking off, so if your safety belts

are fastened?' Lucinda asked, smiling when they had both nodded to affirm that they were. 'Lovely. Flight time should be just under two hours—winds are in our favour and the journey should be smooth sailing.'

With that she retreated before Amelia could get a word out of the partly opened mouth. That delectable, betraying mouth.

I think we should speak to HR.

He couldn't believe the words he'd uttered. Lust-ridden fool. Perhaps that had been her plan after all. To seduce him and—no. Her refusal to speak to HR, her insistence that they never speak of it, her behaviour since Hong Kong, it didn't make sense if that was her plan.

That he had been foolish enough to open the door to any kind of impropriety in the first place was his very own cross to bear. Self-disgust and acceptance—they burned with enough heat to bring pinpricks of sweat to the back of his neck. Alessandro would take whatever punishment he deserved for his transgression. But the sisters' text messages had claimed to have identified proof of corruption.

Impossibile.

Even the word 'corruption' left a bitter taste in his mouth. It was an outrage that this younger Seymore was trying to claim that against them. The audacity of it was simply incomprehensible and while he could concede that there was a certain ingenuity to their plan of attack, it was this—this supposed evidence of corruption—that betrayed the sheer magnitude of their stupidity.

It was simple. Once he had the information he needed, he would ensure that neither he nor his cousin would hear the name Seymore ever again.

Amelia was feeling really quite uncomfortable by the time they disembarked the plane and got into the limousine waiting for them. She had enough sense to know that any more questions would be met with either silence or derision, which had kept her pretty much quiet no matter how strange the situation was becoming. She pressed a hand to her stomach, and although she desperately wanted to turn up the air conditioning in the back section of the sleek vehicle, the thought of attracting Alessandro's attention was worse.

Italy. They were in Italy.

And even though they had left London comparatively early, the travel and time difference meant that it was now midday and Amelia was hot. Everything felt a little damp and stifling. The air between them was thick and heavy, and she had to work hard to calm her breathing.

She had never got over the way that the Rossis travelled continents as if by the click of their fingers. When she'd interviewed for her position, Amelia had known international travel would be expected, which was why she'd not been able to lie about her name. A copy of her passport was held on file by Rossi Industries and she was expected to carry proof of identification with her at all times.

But as she gazed out of the window, trying to ease

the roil in her stomach, the sight of cypress trees in the distance struck her with such a wave of familiarity. The sound of little girls laughing and the scent of sunscreen rose up around her. A warm dry heat hit her skin, turning it rosy in her mind, and the taste of lemon sorbet made her mouth water.

Amelia hadn't been back to Italy since her and Issy's lives had changed for ever. But for just a moment, Amelia wanted to bask in her memories. Her parents enjoying a lazy afternoon beside an azure blue pool in a sprawling villa on the far edges of Capri. Her father's cream linen shorts and brown sandals displaying pale English skin and the mosquito bites their mother used to tease him about. Jane Seymore's smile when she looked at her husband as they had lunch looking out across a stunning sea punctuated by jagged rocky outcrops. Issy's terrible aim as she threw beach balls at her while she was trying—and failing—to get a tan.

She had forgotten it. The last family holiday they'd had before the Rossis had ripped apart everything they'd known, and her heart filled with an old ache she hadn't allowed herself to feel since she and Issy had chosen vengeance.

She felt, rather than saw, Alessandro's attention fix on her. The touch of it so different from the heated *yearning* from the past few weeks that it brought her out of her memories. Now it felt cool and tasted like anger and Amelia began to fear that just maybe he *had* discovered who she was.

Italy, Lexicon, the deal. It could almost have been purpose built for her. She spoke fluent Italian—one of the three languages she had studied in order to embellish her résumé for Rossi Industries. The land—it was similar to a deal RI had rejected about two months before she'd interviewed for her position—a deal Issy had researched to help Amelia with her interview. The sudden change in Alessandro's temperament—she'd seen him under huge amounts of pressure before, right down to the last beats on several billion-dollar deals, and he'd never been *cold*. Clipped, harsh, demanding and exacting to the point of brutal? Absolutely. But there was a heat, drive, a momentum that swept you up and made you want to meet those standards, made you want to be with him in that success. It was…attractive, *alluring*.

Stop!

There was no way that Alessandro could have discovered anything wrong with the deal and she had covered her tracks too well in the company to have been identified as Thomas's daughter. But, oh, God, what if something had happened to Issy? What if Gianni had—?

Her swift gasp of shock drew not just Alessandro's focus, but his gaze.

'Ms Seymore, is something wrong?'

His words, full of grit and gravel, shifted her pulse into a higher gear.

'No, Mr Rossi,' she replied through bloodless lips. She had to know. Picking up the file beside her, she scanned the documents and looked at the memo date from Lexicon to Rossi Industries. Second of June. She managed to stop her hands fisting before the crumpled paper could betray her discovery. It would be highly unlikely to near inconceivable for anyone in Italy to have sent a work memo on *Festa Della Republica*. Italy's Republic Day was a fiercely celebrated bank holiday on which *no one*—bar first responders—worked.

'You put the documents together yourself?'

He nodded, his gaze inscrutable.

Oh, God. He knew who she was.

Amelia Seymore was in serious trouble. And if she was, so was her sister.

Alessandro knew there was a risk that something in the documents could tip Amelia off, but with such little time he'd had no choice. And now, as the limousine made the last twists and turns towards the only place in the world he could have brought her, did it really matter if she knew that she had been found out? Because that had been the only conclusion to draw from the shocked gasp she'd tried to hide.

And in interesting contrast to that momentary betrayal of emotions, the woman beside him seemed unduly calm. He could almost be impressed by her. *Almost.* He looked out of the window before he did something stupid like look at her again.

The opening move of the game had been made. He had brought her into his domain and if she hadn't already, then soon she would realise the reality of her situation. That she was completely and utterly at his mercy.

The thought detonated such a riot of emotions, it infuriated him that Amelia Seymore could be so...*calm*.

The electronic gates at Villa Vittoria parted smoothly and the driver took the fork in the road that would lead to Alessandro's half of the dramatic oval-shaped compound. The other would have taken them to Gianni's half of the unique estate. With near enough two hundred and fifty acres across the entire property the estate was worth more than ten million euros. But it was what lay at the heart of the compound that made it priceless to Alessandro and Gianni.

As the car took the road that swept alongside a large area of land that looked to the world like a pretty wildflower meadow, it was so much more to Alessandro. To him and Gianni, it was what could have utterly broken them, but instead it had become the thing that defined them.

Poppies, cornflowers, daisies and violets covered the stretch of land that Alessandro and Gianni had bought after years of secretly saving every single penny they could. Scrimping and sacrifice had garnered enough money to make the initial purchase, and a savage loan with near-insurmountable interest rates from a highly unscrupulous money lender was to cover the build that would have been their first property.

Would have. Had it not been for Thomas Seymore.

Thomas Seymore had seen Alessandro and Gianni,

two eighteen-year-olds with hope in their eyes and barely enough money in their pockets, and considered them easy targets for his villainy. He had been wrong to underestimate them. And he had paid the price.

And now, it seemed, he had to teach the daughter exactly the same lesson.

So be it.

The car pulled up alongside his half of the estate that bracketed one side of the land that had been sold to them illegally. Oh, they could have tried to sell it on, offloading it onto another poor unsuspecting bastard, perhaps even pay off a surveyor as Seymore had, to ensure that the buyer didn't discover until it was too late that the land was unfit for development. But instead, they'd kept it. As a reminder, not to ever forget the sting of that betrayal, a reminder of just how far they had come. Slowly, but surely, they had bought the land surrounding the little parcel Seymore had sold them and they had eventually turned it into Villa Vittoria, their home and their refuge.

Beside him, Amelia opened the door of the limousine and stepped out, her gaze scanning the impressive vista before her with something like awe. He exited the vehicle and, with a knock on the roof, the driver departed, leaving just the two of them standing on the sandy driveway facing off against each other.

'Why am I here?' Amelia demanded, only a slight tremble in her voice.

'To face the consequences of your actions, *cara*,' he growled in warning.

'Funny.' The word sliced out through tightly clenched teeth. The paleness of her skin serving to highlight the slashes of anger painting her cheeks red. 'I was about to say the same to you.'

CHAPTER FOUR

DESPITE HER FIERY RESPONSE, the sun heated Amelia's skin to the point of discomfort and her mouth was dryer than a desert. During Issy's online investigations, she had found mention of the estate that the Rossi cousins shared, but there were no photographs or plans anywhere online. From the scarce descriptions her sister had been able to cobble together though, it could only be where Amelia was now.

Alessandro had discovered who she was and brought her onto his territory—a move calculated to cause her the maximum amount of disturbance. He clearly thought she was at his mercy. But he had also, clearly, underestimated her.

This was her mess and she had to fix it. Her first priority was to make sure that her sister was okay. The last message she'd had from Issy was a picture she'd sent yesterday of her in a luxurious room on the yacht she'd obtained to lure Gianni Rossi away from contact. Everything in her wanted to grab her phone and call Issy immediately. But she had to play this carefully. Once

she knew that her sister was okay, Amelia would identify exactly what it was that he knew, what he *thought*
he knew, and what damage she could still do. She just
needed to get him talking.

And the best way to do that? Make him think he was
the one in control.

She looked around. In the distance she caught sight
of a wall that ran the length of the estate from what
she could tell. On the far side of the large wildflower
meadow was a villa—similar in design to the buildings
behind her, but with slight differences. She narrowed
her gaze, recognising Gianni's flair for the dramatic in
contrast to the starker, more serious lines of property
that suited Alessandro's personality. But she was surprised that he had chosen to bring her to such a private
place—his *home*.

She shaded her gaze from the midday sun and craned
her neck to look up at Alessandro, who had, once again,
chosen to hide behind his sunglasses. *Coward.* He gestured behind her to a small stone pathway leading away
from the main building. Fighting him on such a small
thing would be foolish. She was going to have to be
very careful and very clever.

They turned their back on the drive and skirted the
edge of the main building. Large trees provided blessed
relief from the Italian sun and in the near distance she
spied what could only be their destination—a low-slung
building beside an azure-blue pool. Floor-to-ceiling gen-

tly tinted windows wrapped around the structure, making it one of the most lavish pool houses she'd ever seen.

Only the best for the Rossis, her sister's voice reminded her.

From here Amelia could just make out a large open-plan kitchenette and lounge to one side and a glass-fronted shower with a half-wall that presumably hid a toilet. Her eyes returned to the shower, where butter-coloured marble stood stark against powerful lines of dark granite. It suited Alessandro to perfection. She could just imagine him hauling himself from the pool, stripping out of his costume and prowling straight into the shower and—

'Is there a problem?' Alessandro asked with faux civility.

She had stopped walking. At some point in the midst of her daydream she had actually stopped walking. She *had* to get better control over herself.

'You mean aside from the fact that you have, to all intents and purposes, kidnapped me and I am now trapped in a foreign country with no money or clothes?'

He notched his head to one side. 'You have your phone?'

'Yes, of course I...'

He held out his hand.

'No. Absolutely not,' she said, punctuating it with a shake of her head.

'No one will help you, *cara*. You are mine until I find out exactly what you've done and how you can fix it, before I remove you from my and my cousin's lives for good.'

'I still think I'll be keeping hold of it,' she said as she pushed past him and continued towards the pool house, hastily pressing the call button for her sister. In her peripheral vision she saw him take out his phone and press a button. Instantly the signal bars on her phone disappeared. What the—?

He had a signal jammer?

'You actually blocked the phone signal?' she demanded.

'Of course. You are a threat and you need to be contained.' Despite his words, his tone was painfully civilised and that, Amelia knew, was when Alessandro was at his most dangerous.

Panic nipped at her pulse, but she ignored it as they reached the pool house, the glass door frame sliding back as if ready for their arrival.

'Would you like some lunch? I had my staff prepare something,' he said as he walked towards the clean, simply designed kitchen.

If he had staff, then…

'*Before* I gave them all the rest of the week off,' he added, as if reading her mind.

A week? Just how long did he plan on keeping her here?

'Oh, I get a meal before you start the interrogation, then?' she threw at him.

'If you like,' he said with a shrug as if he cared little if she ate or starved to death.

She picked at her thumbnail, struggling to play it cool while her mind conjured all manner of scenarios Issy might be going through. She couldn't take it any more. Concern for Issy eclipsed everything.

'I'll not say another word until I know if my sister is okay.'

Alessandro bit back a curse. She was a traitor. A spy. She had done who knew what damage to his company and yet still every single inch of her shone with defiance, the burning heat in her eyes curling around him like a flame. Taunting him. Daring him.

And for the first time in his life, he was at risk of losing his legendary cool. He'd kept himself in check ever since his father had first used his fists on him, determined never ever to become anything like the monster who had provided half of his DNA.

He turned away from her before he did something he'd regret—something that had none of the violence of his father and all of the passion of a lust-filled youth. What kind of spell had she cast upon him? He placed the plates his staff had put together on the table and retrieved a bottle of wine from the fridge. At her raised eyebrow, he simply stared at her.

'I'm less concerned about your sister, and more worried about what she is doing to my cousin.'

Amelia opened her mouth as if to say something but

snapped it shut. She was apparently planning to stick to her word not to say anything until she heard from her sister.

Amelia and Isabelle—sisters and daughters of Thomas Seymore. He searched Amelia's face for signs of the tall, thin British man who had sold them a worthless plot of land all those years ago. He couldn't quite see it. Where her father had been lean and long, his features sharp and harsh, Amelia was petite, softer, *sweeter*. Looks that were clearly deceiving.

He frowned. Perhaps he should have kept an eye on the Seymore family. But he'd thought the business done with the moment he and Gianni visited the old man to let him know that his company was not his own any more. After that, Alessandro had cared only about the harsh lesson they'd learned at the hands of a selfish, corrupt, rich Englishman.

He took out his phone and pressed the button to lift the signal blocker. The technology had been installed as part of the electronic security system designed by Thiakos Securities, one of the best in the business.

'Call her,' he said, with a careless shrug.

Before he'd finished speaking Amelia had her phone pressed to her ear.

Alessandro poured himself a glass of wine as she turned her back on him.

It was no great loss to let her speak to her sister—if anything it would hopefully loosen her tongue enough to talk. *Then* he would uncover just what it was she had sabotaged. Of course, the most logical target would have been the Aurora project. But it could have been anything she'd worked on in the last two years. And that was a lot of projects. Because she'd been so *good* at her job.

He watched a drip of condensation glide from the lip of the water jug and down over the shoulder and remembered chasing a bead of her sweat with his tongue, her cries in his ears and her skin hot and flushed beneath him. It had fallen into the wide valley between her breasts but he'd became distracted by a taut rosy nipple. He'd palmed both breasts as he thrust deeper into her, licking up the salt from her skin and—

The slam of her phone against the table yanked his attention back to the present, his gaze clashing with her mute anger. He pulled at the collar of his shirt and rolled his shoulders.

'No answer?'

She simply glared at him and, for the first time since Gianni had called him the night before, he almost laughed. Here they were, dealing with the highest stakes possible, and she was playing a child's game of silence.

Sighing in frustration, he dialled Gianni's number and listened as a recorded message informed him that the number he was trying to reach was unavailable. Irritation mixed with a touch of concern, he called again even knowing it wouldn't produce a different outcome. Frowning, he tried to reach the captain of Gianni's yacht.

A brief conversation revealed that Gianni and Amelia's sister had just been let off the ship.

'Satisfied?' he asked, hanging up the phone, knowing Amelia had followed the conversation in Italian.

The swift, single shake of her head was expected. If he were in her shoes, he doubted he would have been either. He brought up the search engine on his mobile and searched for #TheHotRossi. The hashtag the press had given Gianni usually made him smile, but not today.

Choosing the images tab, he scrolled through pictures of his sharp-cheekboned, chiselled-jawed cousin and found what he was looking for. A model with her thumbs hooked—supposedly seductively—in the waistband of her bikini had failed to realise that the photographer's gaze had shifted over her shoulder to the couple at the end of a jetty. Gianni's yacht was backing away from St Lovells, the small Caribbean private island owned by Alessandro's cousin, but it was the couple that drew the eye. Long blonde hair had been caught by the wind, a face similar to Amelia's, but different too, staring up at Gianni with so much intensity the photograph felt intrusive.

Unsure what to make of it, he nevertheless slid the phone back across the table to Amelia.

'It was time-stamped less than an hour ago.'

Amelia scrutinised the picture. 'I want to talk to her.'

'I'm sure you do. I've a few things I'd like to say to her myself.'

'You will stay away from her, you beast.'

Alessandro laughed. 'Beast?' he demanded, but it was his eyes that taunted her, reminding her that it wasn't what she'd called him in Hong Kong.

Amelia looked away, needing to hide her illogical reaction. This constant push and pull between them was making her nauseous. Wasn't it why she'd been forced to lie to her sister and tell Issy that she had proof of their corruption? She'd just wanted it all over. The vengeance, the lies, the pretence. Fighting Alessandro, fighting herself. It had been so exhausting and so *hard*.

'You needn't worry about your sister. Gianni is, despite popular opinion, a gentleman.'

'Yes,' she said. 'By all accounts, he's most definitely the nicer of the two of you.'

Alessandro glared at her from across the table. She'd meant what she said though. From all of Issy's research it was clear that, where Alessandro ran cold, Gianni ran a passionate hot, full of charm he used as indiscriminately as he did freely. And a huge part of all of Amelia's plans had been to ensure that her sister would be safe no matter what.

It had always been Alessandro that was the wild card.

She poured herself a glass of water, hastily making and discarding various plans and options. She didn't feel physically threatened in the slightest and she didn't think for one minute that Alessandro would lay a finger on her.

But he had. In Hong Kong. There, he'd touched,

teased, delved with those fingers, bringing her to orgasm again and again and—

She thumped the empty glass of water she'd consumed in one go down on the table. Alessandro watched her with steady eyes as she refilled it, not caring that she looked rattled, she was thirsty and she would drink all the water she needed.

She squared her shoulders, placed her hands in her lap and composed herself. She'd always known that discovery was a possibility. She'd rehearsed this moment over and over in her mind—what she'd say, how she'd answer whatever questions she could imagine him asking. In some ways it was a relief to finally be here and get it over with. 'Interrogate away, Mr Rossi,' she said with a dismissive sweep of her hand.

'What did you do?' His words were clipped, his tone uncompromising.

'You might have to be a little more specific than that, Mr Rossi,' she said, leaning back in her chair, unconsciously trying to put just a little more distance between them. As if he'd noticed, he leaned forward, erasing her momentary reprieve.

'You have done something to damage Rossi Industries.'

She held his gaze, trying to ignore the muscle flaring at his jaw like a warning beacon.

'Well?'

'I believe that was a statement, not a question,' she replied. The flash of anger, a gold lightning strike, was expected but the rumbling thunder of disdain cut her to the quick. Gritting her teeth, she stared at a point just below his chin. The tie of his knot was slightly skewed, as if he'd pulled at it and then tried to twist it back into place.

'According to your sister, you claim to have found proof of corruption.'

Her adrenaline spiked, sending a scattering of stings to nerve endings all over her body.

'But as we both know that is simply neither true nor possible, so there is only one logical conclusion. You have lied; to your sister—maybe even to yourself. An act that is desperate and dangerous and I don't like either of those things. So I ask again, *Amelia*. What. Did. You. Do?'

Stubborn and mutinous, Amelia refused to answer his question. Refused to meet his eye. Refused to engage. But she couldn't deny that everything he said was true. She had lied to her sister, to herself. She *was* desperate and it *had* been dangerous. But if she told him now then it would all have been for nothing.

'You are playing a very dangerous game.'

And finally, she couldn't hold it back any more. 'With rules *you* wrote, ten years ago,' she accused, the words dripping with bitterness and resentment.

'Frankly, Ms Seymore, I don't care. I don't care what you think happened ten years ago, what you think your father did or did not deserve, or what happened to him or you after that.'

Outrage lashed at her soul, in a silent cry of pure injustice. It howled and raged in her chest, wanting out, wanting to cause as much hurt as had been done to her and her sister.

'What I care about is the nearly hundred thousand employees in Rossi Industries and the countless associated businesses that would be negatively impacted by your temper tantrum.'

She gasped. 'Temper—'

'And honestly? It is inconceivable that you and your sister are playing a petty game of revenge for a man who was more corrupt than anyone I know. And given the number of billionaires, businessmen and politicians, that's really saying something.'

He was breathing hard, but not as hard as Amelia. The blood had drained from her face, leaving her worryingly pale, but the sheer force of his anger was still riding him hard. So he missed the genuine disbelief and confusion shadowing her gaze before it was shuttered.

No, all he saw was misplaced outrage and indignation. How dared she? The little fool had put so much at risk he was incandescent with anger.

'You can spare me your lies, Alessandro, there's no gallery here to play to.'

'Lies? *You* talk to *me* of lies?' he accused as he saw his barb hitting home.

'I did what I had to,' Amelia replied, unable this time to meet his gaze.

'With no thought to the consequence of your actions?'

'Why should I have? What more can you do to me? You've already taken *everything*.'

Refusing to let her words needle into his conscience, he pressed on.

'Amelia—I wasn't speaking of you. The consequences of any kind of sabotage will put hundreds if not thousands of jobs on the line, the ramifications for their families could be devastating. Didn't you think of them?'

'No!' she cried, the first real sense of emotion breaking through the façade that she had held in place for two years. 'No. I didn't. I was thinking of my father, who you *broke*. I was thinking of the way he lost not only his business, but his house and his friends and his social standing. It destroyed him.'

He hardened himself against the emotion bringing tears to her eyes that she was too proud to shed. Her loyalty, passion, her love for her father might have been alien emotions to him, but even he would have to have been a rock not to be moved by her. He looked away, out to the edge of the pool and beyond to the piece of land that Thomas Seymore had sold them.

Land that was so unstable it would never have supported the foundations needed for any kind of housing or development. Thomas Seymore's deception had set them back years and thousands of euros and had been a both brutal and harsh lesson. They had nearly broken themselves, working every single hour they could to buy, fix and flip a much cheaper property nearly a hundred miles away from where he now sat with Amelia. He and Gianni had clawed their way, property by property, deal by deal to the point where they had been able to finally mount a hostile takeover of Seymore's own business.

'I remember it, you know. The day you came to our house.'

Alessandro turned his gaze back to Amelia. But there was no indignation in her tone this time, it wasn't strong with conviction. It was the voice of a daughter who had heard things said about her father that she shouldn't have.

'I remember what you said to him.'

The single thread of shame woven into that whole encounter began to unravel deep within him. Alessandro hadn't taken pleasure from that day—in fact it had been precisely that point that had brought him back from the edge of a cliff he'd been far too close to. In that moment, he'd never been more like his own father and Alessandro had sworn never to be that man again.

'Don't,' he said, before she could repeat the words he and his cousin had said that day.

The look she gave him shamed him anew.

'You might not have made him drink, but you put the bottle in his hand. You might not have put him in the ground, but you dug that hole, Alessandro. You and Gianni.'

Angry at the truth of her words, at the events that he had unknowingly started, Alessandro lashed out.

'Amelia, you might be a lot of things, but you're not stupid. Didn't you ever wonder why it was so easy for two twenty-year-olds to take over your father's business? Did you ever think that we shouldn't have been able to do it?'

'Why should I?' she demanded with the blind loyalty of a child. 'He was my father!'

Perhaps it was the differences in their upbringing. Perhaps he might have been the same had he had a father with even an ounce of love in him. But he hadn't, so he couldn't conceive of her naivety. He shook his head, intensely disliking that he was going to have to destroy Thomas Seymore all over again.

'You might not have the proof of *our* corruption,' he said to her, pushing back to stand. 'But you should know that I kept everything about our dealings with your father.'

He walked over to the corner of the living room and retrieved an old faded brown folder from a side cabinet. He returned and placed it in front of her on the table.

She looked up at him, her eyes betraying the first glimpse of doubt he'd seen in her. His conscience told him not to do this. But it was already done.

'Proof of corruption indeed,' he said, looking out to the wildflower meadow. 'How fitting.'

And he left, knowing that she would read the contents of that folder. She wouldn't be able not to. As the sun began to fall, he paced around the large swimming pool, his gaze returning far too often to the female form bent over the table, turning page after page. With her experience at his company, he knew she would easily interpret the sale documents, evaluations, the different surveys. He'd even left the paperwork for the loan in there—he didn't care if she read that. He had no shame about how desperate they had been to agree to the punishing repayment rate, nor how hard they'd worked to pay it back, seeing it only as proof of how far they had come. Their plans, their hopes and dreams…*everything* was in that folder.

He heard the scrape of her chair against the floor and turned. She pinned him with such a look his heart lurched. Or at least he thought it had. Then, as the papers in Amelia's hands scattered, he realised it was her—and he was running before she hit the floor.

CHAPTER FIVE

HER HEART HURT. That was the first thing she noticed. Not the dull pain in her head that kept her eyes closed, or the hot agony in her shoulder that forced her onto her side. It was the ache radiating out from her heart and soul, confusing her momentarily until she remembered.

She turned to bury her face in a pillow so plush and silky soft she wanted to climb into it. A breath left her lips in a shudder and she curled in on herself like a child. But that only made her think of her father. The father she had looked up to, even as he sank deeper and deeper and further and further into a bottle. Even as he ignored his daughters' pleas and his wife's desperation—a wife who would then choose to follow him into a drug-induced oblivion after his death.

In the aftermath of their neglect, Amelia had stepped in to pick up the pieces. To make sure that Issy had a meal to eat after school, did her homework on time. That clothes were washed and bills were paid. She'd had to wrestle money for food from their mother before she could spend it on whatever drug she could find to fill the hole left by her husband's death. And in those horrible early years it had only been the idea of retribution against the Rossis that had kept her and Issy going. It had been her suggestion—their plan of vengeance—and they had clung to it like a lifeline. But she couldn't hide from the truth any more. Page after page in that horrible file had peeled back the scales from her eyes and she had seen. Seen more than she'd ever wanted to.

It had *never* crossed her mind that her father had been corrupt. Never. By the time Thomas Seymore lost his company she had been only fifteen years old. She'd been to his office only twice, his talk of work so boring when her life was full of the exclusive private school she and Issy had attended, piano lessons, ballet, the occasional horse-riding lesson. Until it had been snatched away from her, she had lived a life of blissful ignorance, never truly understanding the depth of her privilege. And when it had been snatched away? She'd known exactly who had been responsible. The two men who had visited with her father that Sunday afternoon.

Just like every week, Issy had prepared the vegetables while she'd made the Yorkshire pudding. The small glass of wine they'd been allowed with the meal had tasted rich and decadent and naughty. And when it had been interrupted, Amelia and Issy had listened at the doorway to their father's office, giggling at the handsome Italian men meeting so importantly with their father. Until the conversation had become harsh and angry.

You are done, old man. Finished. You will never work in this industry again. And if you even think to try, we will make sure that you will regret it.

Everything you thought you had—it's ours now and there is not a thing you can do about it. Any pathetic attempt to crawl back into this industry will be met with swift and significant reprisal. Know that and choose not to test us.

When they had left, Thomas Seymore had looked up to find the eyes of his wife and children on him, having heard the entire exchange. For a man whose pride and standing was everything, the two youths Alessandro and Gianni had been had struck their mark.

Only now, lying there cocooned in luxury once again, the words took on a different meaning—and rather than sheer hatred towards Alessandro and Gianni, Amelia now tossed and turned in the wake their accusations and taunts left behind them. Instead of arrogance and venomous poison, she heard the quake of injustice. Her father had conned them into buying land he knew they'd never be able to build on. He'd not simply seen them as soft targets, he'd purposefully set out to bribe an official to make it happen. How many other times had he done something like that? How many other people had he scammed and conned?

And... *Oh, God. Firstview. The Aurora project. Issy!*

A sob rose to her lips and she tried to cover her mouth with her hand.

'Amelia...'

Her sob turned into a cry of alarm. She hadn't realised she wasn't alone and the thought that Alessandro had witnessed her pain made her feel vulnerable and exposed in a way she'd never experienced before.

'I'm sorry... It's okay, *you're* okay,' Alessandro said, his tone unusually gentle and careful.

She inhaled a shaky breath and turned to find him sitting in a chair in the corner of a room she didn't recognise. He looked...terrible. His shirt was undone at the collar, sleeves rolled back and there wasn't an inch of clothing that wasn't creased or crumpled in some way. The stubble she remembered had morphed into something much more substantial—the beard lending him even more of a forbidding appearance.

'Where am I?' she asked, trying to sit up. Hand out in a gesture for her to stop, he took a breath—nearly as shaken as her own.

'In my home.'

'Not the pool house?'

He shook his head once.

Taking a quick assessment, she realised she was no longer in the business suit she'd worn before. She shot him a look full of accusation and the hand he'd held out shot up in surrender.

'Not me,' he said simply.

'Then who?' she growled.

'My doctor.'

She frowned. She remembered standing from the table, the shock loosening her fingers on the file, the paper dropping and a look of alarm so stark in his eyes that she felt genuinely scared but she didn't know what for and then…

'I fainted,' she remembered. 'You called a doctor?'

'Of course,' he replied, outraged by her surprise—as if she'd accused him of breaking the Geneva Convention. She swallowed, her throat painfully dry. Alessandro must have noticed as he stood from the chair and brought her a glass of water. She had to crane her neck to look up at him, and he stared at a spot beside her on the bed as if not wanting to make eye contact. 'Can you…?'

She nodded, levering herself up against the headboard. She took the glass from his hands, careful not to make contact. She didn't know if that might send her back into a faint.

A knock on the door drew her attention to a little old man with deeply tanned skin and a shock of white hair.

'Ahh, you are awake. Marvellous,' he pronounced, as if she knew exactly who he was and why he would think it was marvellous. 'Alessandro, if you would?' The old man gestured for him to leave and Amelia held her breath. This was her chance! She needed to get out of here.

Once Alessandro left, she took a breath and turned to the old man. 'I've been kidnapped. I'm being held against my will,' she whispered urgently.

'I know, dear,' he said, sitting on the bed beside her,

picking up her hand and patting it gently. 'Alessandro explained everything.'

'Wait, what?' she asked, confused by a response that was entirely the opposite of what she'd been expecting.

'He really is quite lovely, when you get to know him.'

'Alessandro? Lovely?' she asked, truly bewildered.

'Yes, well. You know, aside from...*that*,' the old man said, apparently reluctant to use the word kidnap. 'Now. I need to talk to you about some tests we would like to run to find out why you might have fainted.'

Alessandro sat in the early morning sun, with his head in his hands and his mind completely blank. Instead of the dawn chorus of birds, or the chatter of cicadas, a high-pitched buzz rang in his ears. He'd been awake for nearly forty-eight hours now, having only really caught the odd hour or so the night before as he sat vigil by Amelia's beside. He hadn't reached her in time. She'd hit the floor with an alarming thud, the sound of which would haunt him for the rest of his life.

He'd called Dr Moretti before moving her and only when the man had agreed to come straight away had he allowed himself to breathe. He'd picked her up and carried her straight to this room. Moretti had arrived in under twenty minutes—but the damage had been done.

Alessandro had been plunged right back into a night-mare from his childhood and the horror of waiting for the doctor to come for his mother, lying bruised, blood-ied and broken on her bed. His father's gaze had been full of anger, resentment and indignation, but the whites of his eyes had held only fear. Fear that he'd finally gone too far.

A cold sweat and tremors had racked his body so much so that Moretti had tried to assess him first, but Alessandro had thrown him off in favour of Amelia. Only when the man had started making his assessment had Alessandro begun to calm down.

For a while at least.

Because then had come the questions—about her medical history, any allergies, intolerances, how long since she'd last eaten, was she on any medication. Thankfully he had access to her medical file on his work computer and he'd shared it with Moretti. Having read it, the doctor had declared that, as there was no immediate life-threatening urgency, any further diagnosis could wait until she woke.

Alessandro had been tempted to argue but his mouth had been quicker than his brain. 'What tests?'

'Oh, the usual. FBC, LFT, U and E, glucose, HCG.'

The first he'd recognised from reruns of medical dramas he'd catch late night on TV when he couldn't sleep. But HCG?

'Yes. HCG levels will let us know if she's pregnant,' Moretti had blithely declared.

And that was when Alessandro's mind had gone blank and the doctor had put two and two together much quicker than he and Amelia might have.

It wasn't possible. They had used protection. Every. Single. Time.

Because Alessandro would never have taken such a risk. Never. Alessandro had made a promise to his father—his direct bloodline would end with him. And he'd meant it. He had absolutely no intention of forcing such a heritage on any other poor bastard. What Gianni chose to do was on him. But Alessandro? No, he had been clear about this since the very night that Amelia's collapse had reminded him of; he would never have a child.

He scoffed, laughing bitterly at himself. He'd always thought of it as his decision, as if his will alone were enough to make it so. Now he could see that the sheer arrogance of such a thought was shockingly naïve and ignorant. Because if she *was* pregnant, if there *was* a baby, Alessandro knew that whatever happened from here on out was up to her.

A woman who had hidden her true identity, snuck into Rossi Industries like a spy, determined to prove them corrupt, and, when that hadn't happened, had sabotaged them. And from the little he did know about Amelia? She was excellent. Quick, intelligent, focused, determined. Without a shadow of a doubt, if she had intended destruction, it was assured. And he still had absolutely no clue what she'd done. He had a team of people searching through everything she'd touched, but that could take too long.

He shook his head. Was that really important? They needed to deal with one thing at a time. And first—

Dr Moretti came out into the small courtyard, eyes bright as always. 'It is a beautiful day,' he announced unnecessarily.

Alessandro resisted the urge to growl. The old man had always been kind. Had always been there when his mother or Gianni's mother had needed him, the mean, vicious streak shared by the two Vizzini brothers. An image formed in his mind of the two bitter old men, slowly drinking their vineyard into insignificance. The pure glee in his father's eyes that his direct bloodline might continue made his throat thick with acrid bile.

'*Come sta?*'

'Tired, thirsty, a little confused, but she's better than you from the look of things,' the doctor replied in quick-fire Italian. 'She's asking for you.'

Alessandro swallowed. His heart began to race, his pulse pounding in his ears.

'Take a breath, Alessandro, or *you'll* faint this time.'

He nodded and drew quick and deep, holding it there for a few seconds before controlling the release. And then readied himself for whatever was to come. Even if that meant he was tied for the rest of his life to a woman he could never trust and who could probably never trust him.

Amelia shook her head back and forth. This couldn't be happening.

'I'm on the pill,' she said, looking up at the doctor.

'And I used a condom,' Alessandro said, also staring

at the poor man as if delivering the news of Amelia's pregnancy made it his fault.

'I had a period,' Amelia said, her lips numb with shock. 'I didn't… Oh, God, I've been taking the pill all this time…' The sudden and shocking fear that she might have somehow already hurt the little bundle of cells trying desperately to grow into a tiny human was horrible.

'Please…' Dr Moretti said in a way that clearly requested some calm from the other two adults in the room. 'Firstly, there is no evidence to suggest that continuing to take the hormonal contraception harms a pregnancy. Secondly, no contraception is one hundred per cent assured. It seems this is an instance of…' He looked between Amelia and Alessandro as if trying to gauge the appropriate word, and decided it didn't need clarifying. 'It is possible that, for some women, periods continue throughout the entire pregnancy. You will want to monitor this with your own doctor when you get home.'

Home. A flat she shared with her sister. A sister still hell-bent on vengeance against her baby's father and his cousin. Oh, God, Rossi Industries. Firstview. She pressed her fingers to her mouth, trying to keep the swell of nausea down. It was all too much.

'Water biscuits. My wife swore by them through all four of her pregnancies.'

She glanced up at the doctor and then to Alessandro, who looked as pale and shocked as she felt.

Moretti, realising that there was clearly much to be discussed, announced that he would let himself out and left the two of them alone in a room that suddenly felt stifling. She needed air. She decided that she wanted to get up at exactly the time that Alessandro collapsed back into the chair she had woken to find him in that morning, only a few hours ago when the world had been completely different.

When she wasn't carrying her enemy's baby. Only, wasn't *she* the enemy?

She bit back a groan. It was all so confusing. She lifted the sheet back and swung her legs out, her feet hitting the cold floor with a slap, yanking Alessandro's attention back to her. Or more specifically her legs. Slashes of red appeared across cheekbones that could cut glass, and she looked away, clenching her teeth against the shocking wave of responding arousal she felt at the sheer *heat* in his eyes.

She might have been able to blame a lot of what had happened in the past six weeks on the hormones, she now realised, but not what had initially driven her into the arms of this enigmatic, powerful and, most definitely, dangerous Italian.

By the time she looked back up, Alessandro had found something intensely interesting out of the window to look at.

'Where are you going?' he asked, his voice thick and rough.

'I'd like some air,' she replied, fighting another wave

of nausea that had more to do with guilt than her pregnancy.

The large Alessandro-sized T-shirt hung from her small frame, beneath which was—thankfully—her underwear. The hemline hit her high on her thigh but she decided that modesty and propriety were the least of her and Alessandro's problems.

She stood, testing her strength, and was happy to find that she wasn't as weak as she'd feared. She got to the door of the room, the burning touch of Alessandro's gaze on her the entire time, and realised she didn't know where to go.

'A little help?' she asked, ruefully.

A hand appeared at her elbow and she jerked away from it. 'Not that kind of help. How do I get out of here?' She stood aside to let him pass and lead the way. Beams of sunlight flooded the hallway and she realised she didn't know what time it was.

'How long was I out?'

'The entire night,' Alessandro replied.

She frowned. 'And you?'

'I stayed with you.'

Instinctively she reached out to take his wrist, pulling him round and dropping his hand the moment he looked at where they touched—as if he wasn't sure whether to push her away or hold on.

'Have you slept at all in the last two days?'

He laughed, a single punch of bitterness and incredulity. 'That matters to you?'

Yes, it did, she was surprised to find. Without the line her vendetta had drawn between them, the feelings she'd tried to deny were creeping in. But, clearly, he wouldn't have believed her if she'd admitted as much. Instead, she bit her lip to prevent any further stupidity from escaping and when he turned back to lead her out of the house, she followed in silence.

Step by step, very quickly, Amelia was realising just how dire her situation truly was. As someone whose job was to make assessments, identify problems and present solutions in order to achieve the greatest success, she was under no illusions about her current predicament.

She had nothing—no savings, no inheritance, no security. After their father had passed, they had finally been able to declare bankruptcy, Thomas Seymore's pride refusing to countenance such a necessary but drastic move while alive. Nine years on, Amelia lived in a one-bedroom flat with her sister in South East London. The majority of her—admittedly impressive—salary from Rossi Industries went to pay for her mother's stay at the rehab centre in South America from her very first pay cheque. What wasn't eaten up by rent had gone into the props Issy had needed to grab the attention of the notoriously extravagant Gianni Rossi. Issy had contributed what she could from her salary as an auxiliary nurse at the children's hospital, when she wasn't spending hours online hunting down every single little bit of information she could get on the Rossi cousins. *Everything* the two girls had done had been streamlined to ensure that as much time and finances as possible could be poured into a vendetta she had instigated. And it had all been for nothing.

Because Alessandro and Gianni had done nothing wrong. There had never been any corruption on their parts. They were completely innocent and she had sabotaged the business owned by the soon-to-be father of her child.

As Alessandro opened a door, she rushed out into the courtyard taking huge gulps of much-needed fresh air. Because if their unborn child were going to have any hopes at a better life than either of its parents, then she would need Alessandro Rossi's help. And she had absolutely no idea if he would give it to her.

Alessandro watched Amelia, hands braced against her thighs, bent at the waist, taking giant breaths of the cool morning air. Gone was the perfectly poised controlled employee who had impressed, not just her manager, his board, but himself with her quick, smart, intelligent and controlled approach to the projects. Gone, too, was the passionate, sensual woman with a desire that eclipsed common sense in a way that was only matched by his own.

But all he could think, all he could hear in his head on a loop, was *you're pregnant*. He felt strangely numb, recognising dimly that the shock of it had robbed him of any sense. He was going to be a father.

But the images that word threw at him were not the

kind of loving, doting parent that inspired the kind of loyalty that had driven Amelia to attempt revenge. They were the kind that brought him out in a cold sweat.

He hated that in front of him was a woman in quite obvious emotional turmoil and all he could feel was panic. He looked away as Amelia pulled herself up straight and felt her gaze on him, even though he wished for the world to be anywhere but here in that moment.

'I can't…imagine what you must think of me.'

'I'm trying very hard not to form an opinion right now, because I don't have all the facts and I don't like jumping to conclusions,' he announced while his molars groaned under the intense pressure of his tightened jaw. It wasn't a lie; he was very close to an edge she had driven him to.

'This… I…' She shook her head, words coming hard for both of them, clearly. She took a deep breath, as if she knew that this was important. To him, to her, he didn't know any more, but he couldn't help but admire the strength she drew on to stand before him under the weight of his scrutiny—a scrutiny that had buckled many a lesser person.

'This wasn't part of the plan. Sleeping with you, or the baby.'

His heart pounded in his chest. Her declaration tapped into a question he'd struggled with from the very first moment Gianni had called him. Did he believe her? He studied her, head held high, back straight, shoulders drawn down. She looked like a soldier facing a firing squad, who had spoken her final words. She met and held his gaze, the pale green orbs so open it was as if she'd flung back the shutters and was asking him to look deep within her. Instead, he looked away and missed the slash of hurt that nearly rocked her on her feet.

'It's yours.'

Cristo. That he hadn't even considered any other possibility showed just how powerful a spell she had cast on him. He nodded to convey his understanding but still couldn't look at her. He went to pull at his collar, to relieve the tightness around his throat, only to find that it was already open. Intensely disliking that she might have caught the sign of his discomfort, he moved his hand to the back of his neck, his fingers brushing against the cold sweat that was gathering there with alarming frequency whenever Amelia was near.

Think it through. Be rational, he ordered himself. He had used a condom and even if she had lied about being on contraception, the chances were slim that pregnancy could have been a secured outcome. And after two years at his company, he might not know her—the *real* her— but she couldn't hide the way she thought. He'd seen it in the choices she made, how she approached and assessed a project, the solutions she offered to problems. And at the very least he knew that she would never have created a plan around a possible pregnancy resulting from one single night with him, that couldn't have been guaranteed in itself.

'So Hong Kong was…' he asked, wanting to know.

She shook her head and looked away, a blush rising to her cheeks and the gentle shrug of her shoulder, the fine bones there marked by his oversized T-shirt. It appeared she was as unable to explain that night as he was.

When she looked back at him, she was squinting up at him, the early morning Tuscan sun turning her brown hair into burnished gold, her pale skin into a sunburst as if even the morning were conspiring against him.

'What now?' she asked.

That was a very good question.

CHAPTER SIX

AMELIA FOUND THE KITCHEN. It was bigger than her flat in Brockley and it made her heart thud. The countertops looked like—and most probably were—marble. She and Issy had money growing up. *Before.* But nothing like this. This was…unfathomable.

She ran her fingers across the cool slabs of white, shot through with grey. It would have looked clinical had it not been for the deep brown wooden floorboards and the copper fixtures. There was a large twenty-seater table between the counter and the floor-to-ceiling windows that wrapped around the entire ground floor of the villa's main building. Having worked out the coffee machine and made herself a decaffeinated espresso, she had been too uncomfortable to sit at the table. The thought of Alessandro sitting here to eat, all by himself, it just…it had made her heart ache in a way she tried to ignore.

He had retired to finally get some sleep, but the warning he'd left her with still sounded in her ears.

Do not think of trying to leave, Amelia.

Oh, she wanted to. She wanted to run. Wished she could click her fingers and be back in Brockley with her sister. Which had just made her worry about Issy. What was she doing now? Was she with Gianni? Was she okay?

Feeling a little unbalanced, she made her way to the sunken seating area facing a fireplace—the mixture of modern and new creating a sense of old comfort that was so lovely she couldn't help but sink into the lush leather. Leaning back, she felt something poke into her hip. Turning, she saw her handbag, and inside she found her phone.

It had signal! Alessandro must have forgotten to turn the signal jammer back on. Without thinking, her fingers had hit call on Issy's number. And then she hung up before it could connect.

What would she tell her sister about her pregnancy? How would she explain herself? How could she ever apologise enough for lying to her and setting them on a path of revenge that was so wholly misdirected?

The questions piled up one after the other, making her head swim. It was her fault they were in this mess, but she couldn't afford to wallow in self-pity. She needed to know if Issy was okay, so she hit the call button again. Her heart dropped when an automated response told her the phone was not in use. Unease swept through her, but she reminded herself that Alessandro and Gianni were not the monsters they had thought they were. And while Issy was impulsive and chaotic in the most adorable way, there was only so much trouble she could get herself into.

No. At this point, Amelia really needed to think about the trouble *she* was in. But trouble felt like the wrong word. Because she couldn't use that word and think of the child growing within her.

It had surprised her, really. It had been like the swell of a wave, starting slowly at first but growing larger and larger until it became an unstoppable feeling, gathering momentum and washing aside everything in its path. This immoveable force had whispered into her heart and soul and she had felt utterly and irrevocably changed by it.

She wanted this baby.

It was a knowing, settling deep into her very being— standing out in stark contrast to Alessandro's feelings.

Because she hadn't missed the way he had looked at her. Hadn't missed the accusation in his gaze, or the sense of something deeper, swelling beneath it all like a monster from the deep. He didn't want this, but for some reason she was sure that it had nothing to do with her attempts to sabotage Rossi Industries. And an ache began to form in her chest. She rubbed at her sternum, wondering whether the decaf coffee was to blame, but really she knew. She knew that it was because of what she had seen in Alessandro's gaze. Fear and alarm.

And on some level, she could understand. A child was a huge responsibility. One that would not only change her life but connect her to Alessandro for ever.

It would be all consuming with, or without, his help and it would change the very essence of who she was.

But it could also be a beautiful thing, her heart whispered. One she wanted so much she could scarcely bear to hope for it. A child that she would love and never reject, never subjugate to her own needs. A child that would have so much more of a chance than she and Issy ever had.

Guilt swirled heavily in her stomach. Issy had lost so much, sacrificed so much for a vendetta that she had instigated. Had her mother known? That their father had been corrupt? That he had sold land knowing it wasn't fit for development? That he had conned people—people who had put everything they had into their plans? People like Alessandro and Gianni. So much had been lost to her father's greed. Who would she and Issy have become had they not spent ten years on this path of vengeance? Where would they be now?

Free.

The thought came unbidden to her mind and for such a soft word it hit her with the force of a truck, rocking her to her core.

Standing in the doorway, he saw her sway. The phone he'd seen her use to make a call—probably to her sister—hung listlessly from her fingers. He fought against every instinct he had to go to her. Earlier that morning, he might have. But he'd managed at least four hours' sleep and now he was thinking more clearly.

This woman had committed an act of sabotage against his business. Her motivation mattered little. She had done something to Rossi Industries and before he could even think about her pregnancy, he needed to know what she'd done. Only once that was resolved, could they talk about…

His gaze landed on her stomach, knowing that there would not be any signs of the baby she carried for at least another three months. Instead of letting his thoughts linger there, he took in the rest of her. She was dressed in the clothes he'd put out for her before he'd retreated to his room. Despite the way she had rolled the waistband of the trousers, they still hung a little low on her hips.

He probably could have raided Gianni's compound, fairly sure that there would be some women's clothing left behind by one of his lovers, but the thought of dressing Amelia in another woman's clothes made him faintly nauseous. Instead, he'd found a shirt from years ago, before he'd filled out into the broad shoulders he was now used to. Still large on her, she'd twisted the edges of the shirt into a knot and somehow looked carelessly fashionable.

Desirable.

No. In his mind a hand slashed through his thoughts, sending them scattering. Enough. Ever since the phone call from Gianni, he had been on the back foot. With so much at stake, he needed to take control of the situation.

'Amelia,' he said, calling her attention to him. When

she came out of her thoughts, her gaze cleared enough
to look at where he was gesturing to the table. She returned her phone to her bag and left it on the sofa, slowly
making her way to a table she eyed with discomfort.

'Would you prefer to talk elsewhere?' he asked, not
out of consideration for her feelings, he told himself,
but more for curiosity.

'What, for Interrogation Take Two?' she asked, a
forced lightness to her tone attempting to take the sting
out of her words as she sat on the opposite side of the
table. He eyed her coffee cup with a suspicion that must
have been obvious because she defensively explained
that it was decaf.

He sat down and rolled his shoulders, trying not to
pull at the collar of the shirt he had dressed in. Earlier it
had made him feel in control, but now that Amelia was
dressed more casually, it felt almost puritanical and obvious. As if he were trying too hard to maintain a bound-
ary between them that had already been obliterated.

'Obviously the…' baby '…*pregnancy* changes a lot.
But I need to know what you did,' he said.

Her eyes flared, guilty slashes painting the paleness
of her cheeks a glowing red, and his stomach dropped.

'It's the Aurora project,' she confessed. 'I'm sorry,
if I'd known—'

'Just that? Or are there any other projects that are at
risk?' he interrupted, his thoughts scrambling to damage limitation. The instinct to call his CFO was riding
him hard, but he didn't know if there was more.

'No. Just Aurora.'

He nodded once. 'Is it salvageable?' he asked, a buzz ringing in his ears. It had been a project he'd spent years on. One that would be visible from his father and uncle's vineyard, it was meant to be not only Rossi Industries' crowning glory, but the final twist of the knife in his father and uncle's back.

She bit her lip. Neither lush nor pouty, her mouth shouldn't have been cause for any kind of fascination— but still he noticed the way the top lip line was more straight than curved, the bottom lip marginally fuller than its partner, exposed by the straight white teeth pinning and blooming the soft pink flesh—

Dio mio, he needed to get a grip.

'Have the contracts been signed?' she asked, shoving him back into the conversation at hand.

Before he'd caught the few hours of sleep he'd needed, he'd managed to get a message out to his staff to stop any paperwork going through at all on any project. It had caused absolute chaos, but clearly it had been worth it.

'Have they?' she asked in the face of his silence.

He was tempted to let her stew, but that seemed almost petty now.

'No.'

She breathed a huge sigh of relief, her head falling into her hands, before she swept the hair back from her face and he caught a glimpse of the woman he had worked beside for two years.

She nodded as if to herself. 'It's Firstview. They don't have the capability to see the project through.'

'We would have picked that up,' he said, dismissing her statement.

'I made sure you didn't.'

He scoffed.

She raised an eyebrow and he got worried.

'How?' he demanded.

'They hid it well enough, but I knew what to look for and I erased or covered the things they hadn't managed to hide.'

'You falsified documents?'

'Yes.'

He shook his head in disbelief. They would never have found it. She could have got away with it, and the damage to the Aurora project—the knock-on effect for not only that project's contracts, but their finance repayments, the partnerships, their reputation—it could have bankrupted them. He struggled to fight back the wave of poisonous anger.

'Does anyone else in the company know? Do you have anyone else in the company working with you?'

'No and no,' she replied clearly and without hesitation.

'You did all this on your own?'

'Mostly,' she admitted with some reluctance.

'Your sister,' he realised. 'And what does she have to do with it?'

'She was to distract Gianni and keep him away until the Aurora project contracts are signed. We knew that were the two of you together it was likely you'd uncover something to bring our plan crashing down.' Amelia looked away, unable to meet his gaze.

'Issy doesn't know,' she confessed, guilt and shame eating at her. 'Anything she does…it's…she's innocent.'

Alessandro looked down on her, disgust pouring from him, and it was nothing she didn't deserve.

'Why?'

Amelia could have pretended to misunderstand his question. Remind him she was getting vengeance for her father, but that wasn't what he was asking. Alessandro valued loyalty above all else, it was clear from his work ethics and his relationship with Gianni. She had shamed herself by lying to her sister and involving her in the first place and Alessandro wanted to know why.

A jagged breath tore through her lungs. Could she admit to him that *he* was the reason? That ever since whatever madness had taken over them in Hong Kong, she'd not been able to sleep without dreaming of him? That she'd walk through The Ruby in London, her skin a hair's breadth from fire every single day because she might round a corner and see him? That her heart was constantly running too fast or too slow, depending on whether she had a meeting with him? That after ten years of wanting his destruction, all she wanted was his touch?

She was about to answer but he cut her off with a huff of bitterness. 'Would it even matter if you did answer? I have no idea which Amelia I'd get.'

A frown cracked through the mask she was trying to hastily adopt but his quick gaze snagged on it.

'The perfect employee? The traitor?' he clarified unnecessarily.

But he was wrong. Issy was the one who had adopted a persona, who had made herself into exactly what Gianni liked—half starving herself into a smaller physique, wearing heels for his desired height, dying her hair to his preferred blonde. But Amelia? She had been herself. She hadn't had to change at all because she'd enjoyed her work. Deep down, she could admit to herself that she'd even been thrilled by it. The cut and thrust of it. The success of projects was *her* success. The pleasure she took from impressing the powerful figures in Rossi Industries. No. Deep down, one of the most painful regrets would be that she would actually miss it when she was no longer there.

'The seducer?' Alessandro's question burst through her thoughts.

'No.' The denial rose to her lips before she could call it back. She deserved his scepticism, but their child deserved more. Their baby that was little more than a few cells held together by hope and possibility. A hope that seemed to pour from her soul in an endless stream. 'No,' she repeated, this time with more strength and meeting the storm in his eyes. 'I told you before, that was nothing to do with the plan.'

'And you expect me to believe that?' he all but spat.

'Frankly, I don't expect you to believe anything that

comes out of my mouth ever again,' she admitted and seemed to have shocked him. 'But you have a situation that only *I* can resolve.'

Alessandro went deadly still, his eyes going from stormy to horrified before passing to shock, sending her headlong into an ocean of emotion that she hadn't expected.

'No!' she exclaimed, her hands flying to her abdomen as if to physically protect their child. 'No,' she said, pushing away from the table, the chair screeching against the floor painfully. She walked along the window line to the far end of the table, looking out at the meadow. She knew that there were many options out there and that this wasn't a decision that should be made lightly. But she also knew the truth of her heart, so she turned back to Alessandro and said, 'I'm sorry if I hadn't made that clear but I'm keeping the baby. Whether you're a part of their life or not, I am having this baby.'

He stared at her, his gaze again unfathomable, his silence absolute. It was as if he were giving her all the rope he could in the hope that she might somehow hang herself with it.

'I meant Aurora. I can save Aurora. I *want* to. Please let me help?'

Instead of relief she saw disbelief and it angered her, even though she knew it was deserved.

'I think I'll handle it from here on out,' he replied, his words dripping with disdain.

'Well, good luck with that,' she replied, sarcastically.

'What's that supposed to mean?' he demanded, leaning back into his chair, even though instinctively she knew that he wanted to close the distance, to crowd her, dominate, and Amelia bit back a curse. Why did that set her pulse racing? Why did that determined look flare between her legs and make her ache with want?

She blinked and the moment was gone. While her heart rate settled to something as close to normal as possible, she gathered herself to answer his question.

'You've only two options now. You give up the project or find another partner. Chapel Developments won't touch you—their CEO doesn't like to be considered second best. And yes, you could have another team at RI look through the project to see if they can find an alternative, but you don't have time. The quotes, the projections, the contracts are all time sensitive. With the cost of materials changing near daily, you've got a month, at most, and that's being generous. And you have no one that could vet an alternative partner and do the groundwork to build a relationship that could support the partnership in that time.'

'No one other than you,' he said, zeroing in on her point.

'I know this project inside out. I know the players… and I know the substitutes.'

'You have someone in mind.'

'I do.'

'Who?'

She stared at him as he waited for an answer. This was her only bargaining chip. This was her only chance to make a deal that would force him to listen to what she had to say. To what she *needed* to say. This was the one and only time she would get to set the tone for her future, for their child's future, and if she got it wrong, it would be disastrous for them all.

Dio, she was good. Glorious even. She had been made for the cut and thrust of the boardroom, of his world. Her mind was sharp, her intellect quick, and her confidence? He might not be quite sure about who she was half the time but no, that wasn't fake at all. He was turned on. Not by her body, but by *her* and he hated it. Hated how dangerous and traitorous this woman truly was.

'I will tell you, but I want something in exchange.'

He shouldn't have been surprised, but he was still somehow insulted and disappointed at the same time.

'How much?' He pushed the words through teeth he'd ground together.

She blinked as if shocked by his words and he begrudgingly had to admit, she was a very good actress. But she was an actress that was also going to be the mother of his child. The reminder cut through him like a knife.

'How much what?' she asked through pale lips.

'Money? How much money do you want?'

The shutters came down and for a moment he thought

that he might have it wrong. She turned around and looked out at the meadow her father had sold him all those years ago. She probably didn't even know that it was that particular plot of land and perversely he wanted to keep that from her.

She looked away, her words spoken to him over her shoulder. 'I don't want money. I wanted a…détente.'

'You want to make peace, while holding back the fix to a problem *you* created?' he demanded, wondering at the brass balls on the woman he'd got pregnant.

'I wanted for us to try to start again without all this,' she said, weaving a hand back and forth between them before shrugging her slender shoulders. 'I wanted us to be able to have a conversation about what we're going to do about our child, without wanting to tear each other raw.' There was a helplessness in her eyes that he couldn't deny—fake or not, and he was leaning towards the latter. 'I wanted us to find a way forward that wasn't destroyed by the past, but I can see now that's impossible.'

Her breath caught, the old linen shirt she wore stretched across her chest, and he dragged his eyes away before he could be distracted by her again.

Our child.

Alessandro had done everything he could to honour the promise he'd made his father—he'd been so determined that his direct bloodline would end with him, that he'd never—not even once—allowed for any other possibility. He'd been happy with that. Welcomed it even.

But his child was growing within Amelia Seymore. A real child and deep within him something turned—years and years of determination and belief were twisting and morphing beneath the weight of something else. His child was here and no matter how he'd thought he'd feel in that moment, and he was feeling a lot, it *wasn't* horror. It *wasn't* anger, or disappointment. As scary as it was, it felt something like hope. The hope that maybe he could do better, be better, than his own father. That he could provide his child with more than he'd ever had, with a better life than he'd ever imagined for himself. And now that determination to end his bloodline seemed petty in comparison to the feeling of protectiveness pouring through him with the power of a tsunami.

He looked back to where Amelia stood, shoulders slumped in defeat, breath almost painfully slow in comparison to what it had been only moments ago.

'You want peace? You want to start again?'

Amelia turned, her eyes filled with such hope—hope that was worryingly close to the way she had looked up at him that night in Hong Kong, as if she were half afraid that he'd say no to their one night and half afraid that he'd say yes. Just as it had that night, her gaze had cleared and a truth had come pouring into her gaze.

'Yes.'

Could he do it? Start afresh with her?

He *had* to. She was carrying his child. Their child. And no, he would never trust her. That bond had been broken irrevocably. But that didn't mean they couldn't at the least be cordial. Whatever happened, he would ensure that his child grew up in a world nothing like his own childhood. He would do whatever it took.

'Who?' he demanded, forcing to push through the exchange, because his first goal was to make sure that Rossi Industries didn't fall because the mother of his child had sabotaged it.

'I don't think you're going to like it.'

'There's a lot that I don't like at the moment. This will be the least of it, I'd imagine.'

She had the grace to look away.

'Who?' he demanded again.

'Sofia Obeid.'

He pinched the bridge of his nose. 'Amelia,' he said, not knowing whether he was cursing her or begging her.

'I know what you think of her,' she said, her hands gesturing for patience or peace, he wasn't sure which. 'But hers is the only company with the capital to help see Aurora to fruition within the timeline and without incurring incredibly painful financial penalties.'

He glared up at her, frustration and intense irritation coursing through him. Sofia Obeid had a reputation for being incredibly difficult and impossible to work with. Not that RI would know as she had refused to take a meeting or even a phone call from the Rossi cousins before now.

'What makes you think you can get a meeting with her?'

'Because I can,' she replied simply.

He scowled as he took in the way the sun streamed in the window and slipped through the linen shirt to outline the subtle curves of the woman not only carrying his child, but who had clearly been sent to test him to his very limits.

'Please. I want a chance to fix this, but I also want a chance to start again,' she said, courage and something like hope shining in her eyes. 'A chance for our child to have more than we did.'

And he was helpless to refuse. 'Okay. But before we do anything, we need to get you some clothes of your own.'

CHAPTER SEVEN

ALESSANDRO WOULD USUALLY have driven himself, but he needed all his wits around him with Amelia present, so had reached out to the driver he kept on staff. In the distance he could see their destination, the city of Orvieto, sitting on a large stretch of rock rising dramatically and almost vertically from the surrounding landscape.

While they were out, his staff would air the main part of the house and fill the kitchen with whatever they might need for the next week and disappear as if they'd never been there. No matter what she said about wanting to rectify her sabotage, Alessandro wanted to keep the people Amelia interacted with to a minimum. He still couldn't be sure that she was telling him the truth.

Liar.

He refused to acknowledge his conscience's taunt. He disliked that her desire to make amends had softened his response to her, but her solution? He pressed a closed fist lightly against his mouth. Sofia Obeid. Of all the people that Amelia could have offered up as a new partner on the Aurora project, why did it have to be the one woman who had refused until now to give them even the time of day? Alessandro and Gianni had considered and discarded her before the start of the project because of that. Amelia wasn't wrong—she was their best option, and if Amelia could get Obeid to sit down with them then who was he to argue?

Alessandro wanted to speak to Gianni. But he'd tried his mobile again last night and couldn't get through. Deep down, Alessandro knew that he could have tried to reach him on St Lovells, Gianni's private island, but what would he have said? That he'd not only opened them up to sabotage, but he'd managed to get their enemy pregnant? He didn't need to speak to Gianni about the project because he knew what his cousin would say. *Do what you need to do. And get it done.* Alessandro didn't need Gianni's permission—he needed absolution.

Amelia sat in the car beside him, picking at the bed of her thumbnail, and he wanted nothing more than to slap her hands apart and tell her to stop. Because the sign of deep worry made him feel like a monster. Because…his mother had used to do the same exact thing, each night while she waited for his father to come in from the vineyards. But he was nothing like his father and she was nothing like his mother. Amelia Seymore was hardly an innocent in all this.

Her mobile phone beeped and he resisted the urge to try and check the screen in case it was a message from her sister. Instead he looked out of the window as they

drew closer to the city famous for the defensive walls
built from the same rock on which it sat, the stunningly
beautiful duomo with its striking white and green façade, and some reasonably decent wine. Certainly, better than anything his father and uncle had produced on
their vineyards.

*I don't care if your fingers are bleeding or your back
hurts. You will not stop until these grapes are harvested,
do you hear me, boy?*

'Alessandro? Did you hear me?' Amelia's soft voice
punctuated the hold his memory had on him and he
turned to look at her. A shadow passed across her face
before she turned back to her phone. 'Sofia has agreed
to meet. But the window is tight. She says she is considering a similar proposition—'

Alessandro scoffed. 'Doubtful. There is nothing remotely similar out there to Aurora.'

Amelia nodded in agreement. 'She's willing to meet
us in Marrakesh tomorrow, but she has warned us not
to get our hopes up.'

'Playing hard to get?'

'Most definitely. She's interested but cautious. His-
torically her company has partnered with those with a
longer track record than RI.'

'What makes you think this will work?' he asked,
genuinely curious.

'Because she will respect who you are and what you
have done,' she replied.

'Why? You didn't?' he said, his tone darker than he'd

intended. He hated losing his legendary control around her. Her compliment—intended or not—had grated, but not as much as the way she simply took his harsh retort as her due. Feeling disconcertingly mean, he was about to apologise when their driver pulled to a stop at the pedestrian area within Orvieto's walls.

Instinctively after exiting the car, he came around the vehicle to open the door for Amelia. She was back in the clothes she'd travelled to Italy in and, despite the slight creases, she looked composed and collected. The way she had looked to him for the two years before Hong Kong. Because after? After Hong Kong, all he'd seen was lust and want and need.

Shaking off the thought, he saw her eyes soften as she looked into the old town in Orvieto.

'What?' he asked, curious to see the city through her eyes.

She gazed up at him, the answer on the tip of her tongue, but looked away as she answered him in a small voice. 'We talked about coming here—my family— when I was younger.'

He tried to temper the anger that rose in him at the mention of her family—of her father. What was it about this woman that pushed buttons that had lain dormant for years? She cleared her throat as if aware of the impact of her words and slowly made her way towards the open square in the heart of Orvieto. He watched her go, letting her rebuild her armour piece by piece—because he *wasn't* a monster.

Catching up with her a few moments later, he gestured with his head towards the shopping district where Gucci sat next to Ferragamo, Dolce and Gabbana rubbed shoulders with Tom Ford.

Her steps slowed, pulling his attention back to her.

'Something wrong?' he asked, his patience wearing thin.

'I can't… These shops…' She stared at them with an expression that somehow merged shame and embarrassment. 'I can't afford them,' she concluded on a whisper.

Fury etched his body into hard lines. He closed the distance between them in a stride, letting loose only a fraction of the anger that was almost constantly simmering beneath the surface whenever she was near.

'What game are you playing now?' he demanded.

Confusion blew her eyes wide open. 'I don't know what you mean—'

Outrage poured through him. He'd given her the détente she'd asked for, he was trusting her with so damn much and she was *still* trying to pull the wool over his eyes. 'I know exactly how much I pay my staff, so don't try the "poor me" pity act,' he forced out through clenched teeth.

Amelia took a step back from the overpowering wave of his frustration. Nostrils flaring and breathing hard, Alessandro looked pushed beyond an edge she'd never even seen him close to and that she had done this to such a powerful man filled her with shame, but also with an anger to match his own.

So instead of backing down, she stepped forward, stealing back some of that righteous indignation that had fuelled her for years.

'Yes, you pay your staff very well, Alessandro, but how many of your staff have student loans to pay off?' She jabbed an angry finger at him that he stared at in outrage. 'How many of your staff have to pay not only for their own needs but those of their sisters?' She stepped into him again, losing some of the control that restraint had given her. 'How many of your staff have to pay for their mother's rehab facility in South America? How many of your staff had to be a parent to their own mother and father when they were just fifteen years old?'

The shock in his gaze cut through her fury and she realised what she'd just revealed. She pulled back her hand, covering her mouth and shaking, and turned away. She heard the approach of two tourists so she crossed the cobbled street to lose herself in a shop window displaying an inconceivable amount of fridge magnets.

She forced herself to calm down—it wasn't just her any more that she had to think of. But the venom in his tone—the anger. They would *never* get past it. How on earth was she supposed to raise a child with a man who hated her?

How do you even know he wants to?

'I didn't...' His voice behind her was thick and rough,

like the crunch of gravel. He cleared his throat. 'I didn't know.'

'Isn't that the point?' she asked, feeling helpless. 'I believe you said that you didn't want to know or care.'

He had the good grace to look about as shamed as she'd seen him—which extended to the clench of a jaw she wanted to soothe, and the fisting of his palms she wanted to release. Seeing him anything other than determined and powerful felt wrong somehow, as if she'd caught a glimpse of a vulnerability that few saw.

He took a breath—for patience or strength, she couldn't tell—and it emerged from his lips on a sigh that she felt gently against the nape of her neck.

'Are you hungry?' he asked, his tone an awkward shade of gentle.

She nodded and let him guide her away from the shop window, down the cobbled street, and towards a little café with seats overlooking the city walls and down into the stunning patchwork quilt of fields interspersed by the tall, thin cypress trees that made it look so different from England.

She ignored the exchange of Italian between Alessandro and the manager, who seemed desperately eager to find them only the best table in the café. She ignored it because she was numb.

Because she realised what she had been doing—that she had been trying to distract herself from the fact that she was having a baby with a man who hated her. That she was about to have a child that would look to her to show them how to be, how to behave, how to see the world and how to love. And she didn't want that child raised in anger or arguments. She didn't want that child raised in struggle, or instability, as she and Issy had been.

Alessandro appeared at her side, and she let him guide her by the arm to the small, white-cloth-covered table. She took a seat as the waiter poured ice-cold water into their glasses and disappeared. Not once had Alessandro looked at her since they arrived.

'We can't keep at each other like this.'

'No, we can't,' he agreed.

Amelia looked at her hands, at the bitten skin around her thumb, knowing that it was a sign of distress and worry. Their baby deserved more than this. She wanted Alessandro to understand her. She needed him to know where she came from and what had pushed her to do what she had done. Only then might they have a chance to move on from the hurts of the past.

'I… After my father lost the business,' she explained, 'he wouldn't work for anyone else. He was a proud man, but no longer had the capital or will to start over. Whatever income he had went into pretending that we hadn't lost everything, for a while at least. My parents spent more money in those first months than I think they had when they'd had the financial security to do so.'

'That is unforgivable.'

She might deep down agree, but there was still a large part of her that wanted to defend her parents, wanted—needed—to see them as the victims. Because if they hadn't been, then how could they have allowed what happened next?

'It wasn't long before we were forced to sell the house. To downsize. We moved to a different area in London, to a different school where Issy and I didn't fit in. Without his money and largess, the people Dad had thought of as friends soon lost interest. Mum became bitter and Dad became mean. His drinking got out of hand and the physical and financial toll was irreparable.

'I tried to keep the worst of it from Issy, but by that point she was old enough to see what was going on. It's a miracle that she didn't veer off the rails and rebel.'

Alessandro was beginning to suspect it was less to do with miracles and more to do with Amelia and the strength she had to keep what was left of her family together. 'And your mother?' he couldn't help but ask.

For the first time since he'd known her Amelia actually looked defeated. 'She never recovered. She loved him so much, but she had also loved that lifestyle and without either she just gave up. She started leaning on anything that would help her escape the reality of her new life.'

Her words shattered something old and brittle deep within him, resonating with the exact frequency he had felt himself. He knew what it was like to be let down by not just one but two parents and while he would never, *ever*, blame his mother, nor would he forgive her her betrayal. Because if she had kept her word, then the world would be a very different place right now. He opened his mouth to say something, to try and reassure Amelia as he'd never been quite able to reassure himself, but she continued.

'It was…difficult, trying to make sure Issy and I had what we needed. But we made it happen.'

Amelia left a lot unsaid, but he could imagine her struggle had been incredibly hard, fighting her mother at every turn. He could see how she had become the head of the family and how, just in the way she described it, she had done so without question or complaint. Perhaps it hadn't even occurred to her that she shouldn't have had to. And against his will he felt guilt. Guilt over his involvement that had left two children so vulnerable.

'And we had you.'

Her words surprised him.

'You and Gianni became a focus for us. Became something that drew us together and drove us forward. Our need to avenge our father gave us strength even in the darkest of times. While our mother wallowed, we used our thirst for revenge to get us up in the morning and keep us going. And while I am truly sorry for what I have done to Rossi Industries, I…we…needed it.'

In her eyes, he saw only truth and he couldn't stop the understanding blooming in his chest. He knew how strong that drive and purpose could be, the power it could provide, but he still struggled with what could have happened to Rossi Industries and the thousands of people employed there.

'Is that why you thought we were corrupt?' he asked.

She bit her lip before answering. 'I needed you to be. Because I needed to blame someone—anyone—that wasn't the two people who were supposed to be… my parents, my guides, my role models.'

Once again, her words and his childhood began to fold together and he wasn't sure how to feel about it. He sighed and gave up the urge to fight the sympathetic feelings trying to emerge.

'I understand. If I'd had someone to blame for my parents' misdeeds, I would have,' he admitted. Something flared in her gaze. Surprise, shock…that indefinable thing that had sparked one night in Hong Kong and had yet to blow out.

Connection.

Alessandro batted the errant thought away, instead focusing on the fact that she had given him something, and he felt the unaccountable need to meet her in kind. But could he do it? Gianni was the only other person on the planet who knew where they came from, the rest of the world believing that the Rossi cousins were placed on this earth as fully formed, financially powerful property gods.

'This wasn't supposed to happen,' he admitted, opening his hand to the skies.

'You and me, or me and…'

'Both?' he admitted, even as a fist twisted his gut and

something close to pain roared in his body to take the words back, as if it were sacrilege to say such a thing to the woman carrying his child. He could see that his words had struck her just as hard and hastened to explain, even when speaking of his childhood was the last thing he'd ever willingly talk about.

'My father was…*is*…he *still* is…a despicable man. He is mean, violent, prejudiced, ignorant and vile in the worst ways. And he doesn't have an alcohol addiction to excuse it.' His voice was rough, scratched out from hatred and hurt. 'Gianni and I grew up on a vineyard in Umbria. I am assuming you know this?'

Amelia nodded. 'You and Gianni have never tried to hide your beginnings. And even if you had, Issy would have found it.'

'I'm beginning to think we might have employed the wrong Seymore,' he said, genuinely impressed by the accurate and detailed research Isabelle Seymore had seemed to gather. He was momentarily distracted by the slight curve of Amelia's lip, her pride in her sister something he respected and understood.

'No, we're not ashamed of our humble beginnings, but we don't like to think on it much. It wasn't a nice place to grow up for either Gianni or myself. We certainly don't talk about it.'

'Then why are you talking about it now?'

'Because you need to understand where I'm coming from as much as I needed to understand you.'

She nodded, slowly, that connection again becoming stronger between them.

'Vizzini Vineyards produces a really quite disappointing Sangiovese. My father and his brother have neither the patience nor the interest to produce anything but. The ground is hard and barely fertile, and my father and uncle too stubborn, too mean and too lazy to do anything about it.

'But every day they go out there and ravage the land and vines as if they might actually one day produce something that would be half decent and make them rich beyond their wildest dreams.

'It will never happen,' Alessandro stated adamantly. 'But that didn't stop them from forcing Gianni and me to work ourselves to the bone.' He huffed out a bitter laugh. 'You want to know why we're so successful? Yes, we're hungry for it, yes, we're determined, but what puts us above everyone else? We were born breaking ourselves; it's in our blood, not by nature, but by nurture. Our only saving grace was our *nonna*. She was the only person that could still the hand of my father and his brother. She was devastated by her sons' abuse and helped us as much as she could, protecting our mothers and us. It is why we chose her maiden name as our surname.'

His eyes softened, making him look so utterly different from the man that ruled boardrooms with an unquestionable authority and conviction, that seared ineptitude away with a single look. This was a youth who had loved and hurt, who was soft and warm. Gianni and Alessandro could have easily each taken their own mother's maiden name. But they had chosen someone who had loved and tried to protect them, they had chosen something that bonded them together as a family, perhaps even closer than brothers, despite only being cousins.

But then his face darkened, as if a cloud had covered the sun.

'She passed when Gianni and I were eight years old.'

His loss was so palpable that Amelia wanted to reach for him, but he had waded too far into the waters of his memories.

'After that, there was nothing holding my father and uncle back. They treated us little better than slaves, working the fields and the machinery during the day, and being their punching bags at night.'

'What about your mother? Gianni's mother?' she asked, unconsciously echoing his earlier question to her.

Alessandro looked away. 'Mine was unable to help,' he said, the simple words concealing so, so very much. 'And Gianni's story is his own.' He shook off her question and turned back to the table.

'My father used to say, "The Vizzini name is all that matters." He was obsessed with it. Every single day, he would say, "It will live on for generations to come." And I promised him, the day that I left, that the Vizzini name, the blood in his veins…it would end with me. It is—*was*—the only vengeance I could take against him.'

He said it looking deep into her eyes, opening himself to her so that she would understand, that she would know the truth—the depth of his promise. And she did. She knew the power of such a promise. Her heart ached for the boy he had been but it also ached for the child they had made together and the future that she had barely hoped for that was beginning to disappear like sand on the wind.

'But now that promise doesn't matter,' he dismissed. Eyes that had been so expressive moments before, so free with their emotions, shuttered, the barrier falling between them with shocking speed and ferocity. 'The child will never even hear of the Vizzini name if I have my way.' There was a determination that she had never seen from Alessandro darkening his words to a level that sounded almost threatening, but not. Amelia realised that it was more like an oath or a promise.

'I need you to hear this and know this.' He pinned her with a steady gaze that she couldn't look away from. 'Our child will not want for anything. *Everything* I have is theirs. I don't know what the future holds for us, but no matter what—our child will be protected from anything it is in my power to protect them from.'

Amelia's heart pounded in her chest. The vehemence in his words, his promise, wrapped tightly around her, but rather than suffocating, it was comforting. A fear that she hadn't realised she'd had eased. Yes, she'd

known that she could find a way to provide for herself
and her child alone if she'd needed to. Issy would have
helped without question. But Issy—bright, beautiful
Issy—deserved more, she deserved not to be held back
by family vendettas or obligations.

But what did his promise mean for her? Did he want
to raise their child together? Did he want more? The
thought of sharing a family with Alessandro, of sharing that responsibility, of working together to care for
their child without fighting, bickering or mistrust…
That was something that lived in a fantasy tied deeply
to one night in Hong Kong that she couldn't yet bring
herself to name.

She knew Alessandro was still angry, and he clearly
didn't trust her, both of which he had a right to. But
Alessandro was also a man who loved his grandmother,
who was loyal to his cousin beyond all else. She knew
and appreciated the tenets he lived by. She knew *him*.
He was a good man.

That was why she'd been forced to lie to Issy, who
would never have embarked on their plan unless Amelia had promised her proof of that corruption. Because
Amelia had known, even then, that there was no proof.
That this strong, powerful, proud and determined Italian would never have done such a thing. So she had
launched them into their vendetta in a bid to be free of a
man she was hopelessly and irrevocably falling for. She
bit her teeth together to force back her feelings again.

Because wanting a man who would protect her the

way he had promised to protect their child—the way no one had ever promised to protect *her*—was a hope too far. Willing back the wet heat pressing against her eyes, she could at least hope for something smaller. If she could help him save the Aurora deal, she could hope for a place to start at least.

CHAPTER EIGHT

As THE PLANE banked into a hard turn, steeply angling
the private jet, Alessandro felt his stomach drop. He
looked across the cabin to where Amelia accepted a
glass of orange juice from the air steward with a smile
that did things to him. He'd checked with Dr Moretti
three times that it was safe for Amelia to fly at this stage
of her pregnancy. The concern he felt for her, the *possessiveness*, had shocked him. For years he'd been determined to ensure that his father's blood ended with him.

But now? Now that Amelia was carrying his child,
when his mind wandered it went to a place where there
was a dark-haired child wrapped safely in their mother's
arms, where there was an uncle who looked like Gianni
who would spoil that child rotten, where there was a
bond between him and a woman he had never imagined
for himself that looked very much like Amelia Seymore.

But when he opened his eyes, there was a company
he needed to save from damage done by that very same
woman. He had meant what he said to Amelia the day

before. That he would give their child whatever they needed, but…

I want a chance.

He cast another gaze to where Amelia sat poring over documents at the table. He'd spent half the night reading the same material the Aurora team had sent over while they'd been in Orvieto. They had returned to Villa Vittoria after a shopping trip that had been less than easy. Apparently offering to pay for it hadn't made things better, only worse. The only thing that had forced her through the doors of the clothing store where Amelia had bought everything she needed was the prospect of meeting with Sofia Obeid in three-day-old clothes.

They had been nearly done when the shop assistant guided Amelia to the lingerie section.

Monk indeed.

Lace, straps, belts, hooks, bows, ribbons, ties… *Cavolo.* It wasn't as if his fevered imagination needed any more to think about. There hadn't been a single night since Hong Kong when he hadn't woken up in a cold sweat relieving none of the fire of want and need in his body. And last night had been the worst yet. As if the knowledge that she was carrying his child had suddenly made everything so much more intense.

He looked out of the window cutting off any curiosity as to what she was wearing under the cream silk shirt that should be conservatively respectable had he not seen the lithe body beneath it. *Cristo*, what madness was this? And why—all of a sudden—was he fas-

cinated by little buttons? A row of them at each wrist
and another row at the nape of her neck leading all the
way down the back of her top to where it tucked into a
pair of wide, high-waisted navy trousers.

Sophisticated. Attractive.

They made her look confident. He hadn't realised
how much he'd missed seeing her like that, until that
very moment. That he was making her less somehow
stirred his conscience and reminded him of things he
never wanted to think on.

He cleared his throat. 'Talk me through the meeting.'

He knew the plan but he needed something to focus
on that wasn't Amelia, their child and their future. Especially when all it made him do was think about his past.

A villa had been booked at the hotel where Obeid
had suggested they meet. Harrak Marrakech was a
fourteenth-century palace set amongst twenty-eight
acres of orchards that opened out towards a view of the
snow-capped Atlas Mountains. Comprised of deluxe
villas, each with private pools, gardens, a private chef
and personal staff on hand twenty-four hours a day, it
was a very impressive hotel, even to Alessandro who,
amongst the sprawling property empire, owned several
of his own with Gianni.

While the car took them from the airport to the hotel,
Amelia talked him through the changes she'd made to
the pitch document in order to cater specifically for
Obeid. He agreed with most of the changes, made a few
tweaks, and left her to make the required amendments,

trying to ignore the fact that this was beginning to feel very much like the trip to Hong Kong.

'She will expect you to do the talking, and she may be offended that Gianni isn't there with you, at the meeting,' Amelia warned as she got out of the car and waited for him to join her. His gaze caught on features he'd once thought plain, which he now knew beneath their subtlety to be exquisite.

He nodded in response to Amelia's statement, knowing that the world was used to the Rossi cousins being two halves of the same whole. Dammit, *he* was used to it. But he had to keep a lid on the irritation lashing at him, needling him, if he had a hope to claw any success back on this project.

He looked up at the building that had quaintly been called a villa and even though he had some of the most impressive buildings in the world under his company name, *this* was incredible.

'Is…is this okay? Sofia would expect you to stay in the most expensive accommodation. Anything less would be either insult or—'

'Weakness,' Alessandro concluded, agreeing with her choice of villa.

A uniformed staff member opened the door to their villa and beckoned them in. A second staff member waited in the marble hallway with two trays, one with glasses of champagne, cool, refreshing orange juice, or water, and the other with dainty pastries, bright with sprinklings of either paprika or pistachio, salty or sweet.

He thanked the staff, listening with one ear as their private concierge informed them of the suite's amenities, while the majority of his attention was spent taking in what could only be described as paradise. He felt Amelia's wary gaze on him like a tentative caress, and in a blinding moment of clarity he realised, that was it. *That* was what was irritating him so much.

There had been no hesitation in Hong Kong, there had been no timidity, nothing held back at all. She had met him touch for touch, taste for taste, thrust for—

'That will be all,' he said, cutting off the staff mid-sentence, knowing that he sounded insufferably rude, but he was being driven to distraction from wanting something that he couldn't allow himself to have. Before he could do any further damage, he turned on his heel and disappeared into his room.

Amelia looked out at the incredible view of the Atlas Mountains, more perfect than any picture. In the garden, a long narrow pool led towards an ornamental arch to reveal the majestic snow-capped peaks in the distance. This was a luxury like she had never known or seen before.

The villa alone had more rooms, bathrooms, and living areas than she could conceive of and that didn't take into consideration the subterranean pool and steam room. She looked over her shoulder at the dark wood table polished so that it was almost a mirror, sprawled with paperwork, charts, workflows, and research on

Sofia Obeid. But what she really saw was the heated look in Alessandro's eyes after he dismissed the staff.

She had seen the face of the man she had spent a night with in Hong Kong. The man who had broken through every single barrier she had wedged between them, the man who made her want to give everything up for just one of his touches, one of his kisses.

She laughed quietly at herself. Back in Italy she had thought she only wanted, and had only negotiated for, a fresh start. But she couldn't afford any more lies. Not to others, or herself. She wanted more. A yearning in her heart, so deep, that only peeling back the layers of her desire for vengeance had revealed it, exposing that raw need to the air.

She wanted *him*.

She wanted to feel alive in the same way that she had that night in Hong Kong. She wanted him to look at her the way that he had that night. Not with anger, or distrust, but something like wonder. As if he'd been as surprised as she, that it was happening, that it was possible to feel that way... It had created an addiction in her. It was the only way to explain it. This constant craving coursing through her veins, travelling throughout her entire body, enslaving it to a need that felt unquenchable.

Focus.

She had to focus. It was imperative that this meeting was successful, that the damage that hung above Rossi Industries like the sword of Damocles—a sword *she* had put there—was removed. Only then would she be able to meet Alessandro on a level playing field. But in some ways, she also wanted to delay that moment. Because she could feel it on the horizon; building between them, getting bigger and bigger and harder to ignore. A storm, a reckoning, that she both wanted and feared.

Alessandro appeared in the arched doorway on the opposite side of the exquisitely decorated living area. If he was trying to hide his thoughts, he'd failed because she could easily read the intensely erotic images in his mind. Goosebumps broke out across her skin. Every single line of his body was drawn with tension, and more. The more that called to that secret place within her. A place that he had imprinted himself on, making sure that she would never be able to think of another man in the same way.

Amelia clenched her hands, his gaze drawn to the movement, and as he took a step forward she instinctively took a step back—halting him mid-stride. He'd opened his mouth as if to speak, when the villa phone's ringtone sliced the air between them.

Blindly she reached for the handset built into the wall beside her and listened to the voice on the other end.

'Yes… Absolutely… We look forward to seeing you soon.'

She placed the handset into the cradle on the wall and looked up to find Alessandro staring studiously out of the window.

'Sofia Obeid is on her way.'

He nodded without sparing her a glance.

* * *

*Get your damn head on straight, right now, or you're
going to lose everything you and Gianni have worked
so damned hard for.*

Amelia instructed the private staff to provide re-
freshments and drinks in the shaded courtyard in the
villa's garden. Covered by a pergola dripping with extravagant fuchsia blossom and rich green leaves, the
courtyard edged a pool that reflected the mountains in
the distance. It should have been peaceful, serene even,
but Alessandro was on edge—a feeling he disliked intensely. Inviting Sofia Obeid into the villa felt personal,
invasive. Again, that protective instinct rose in him,
surprising in its intensity, wanting to keep this place,
and Amelia, to himself. And it shook him to his core.

Presently she was fussing over the table in a way
that reminded him of the day she had helped to pitch
for Firstview, the day she had tried to sabotage his company. And he was trusting her to save it? This could
just as easily be another trap. He pushed the thought
away, searching for a calm that was far from natural,
but successful nevertheless.

He grounded himself in facts, in the presentation, in
the confidence that it was a sterling project that would
be more than just a roaring success. In the belief that
Obeid would see this and partner with them—even if
it was a partnership born from desperation rather than
choice.

Amelia looked up as if she'd felt the change in him.

Awareness flashed in her golden green gaze, before she looked away. They heard the knock on the door, the villa's staff greeting their visitor, and Alessandro turned to welcome what would either be their salvation or damnation.

Sofia Obeid was a very attractive woman. Six feet of sheer elegance and beauty did nothing to distract from the lethal intelligence in her sharp gaze. Despite her reputation for being impossible to work with, Alessandro could at least appreciate her exacting standards. And though there had been whispers of impropriety, Amelia had assured and reassured him that she had found not one single ounce of evidence pointing to the truth of it. And given how ruthlessly she had investigated him, Alessandro was almost sure that that was what they were—whispers.

'Ms Obeid. Thank you for meeting with us. I know that it was both short notice and inconvenient for you.'

Her eyes narrowed momentarily, as if she was surprised that he was so openly acknowledging his need for her visit.

She hates obsequiousness with a passion. Be simple, be honest, be direct, Amelia's coaching whispered into his mind.

Sofia nodded once, glanced at Amelia, who bowed her head in a way that surprised Alessandro, but seemed to satisfy Sofia.

'Would you care to sit?' he asked, gesturing to the table.

'Thank you,' Sofia replied in a precise English accent that spoke of her years of private schooling in Britain.

She sat in the middle seat, gesturing for him and Amelia to take the chairs either side of her.

'Where is the other one?' she asked when they were all seated at the table.

'The other—?'

'The *Hot* Rossi?'

Alessandro just about managed not to choke on the coffee he'd just taken a sip of. The unconcealed disdain of Sofia's tone making his cousin's moniker somehow amusing. He was about to come up with a lie, when a warning flashed in Amelia's gaze. A warning Sofia might or might not have seen.

'He is in the Caribbean.'

'You expect me to take this business deal seriously while one half of Rossi Industries suns himself and his ego on a beach, presumably—if reports are true—surrounded by as many women as he can get his hands on?'

'I do. My cousin might—' he saw the flash of scepticism in Sofia's gaze '—*does* have a reputation, but he works harder than anyone else I know. He earns his one holiday a year, each and every other day in the office. And as you—and the world—have noted, we are effectively one and the same. If I speak, it is for the both of us, unquestionably. And I promise you, if he could be here, he would. It is not a reflection on how much we value your time and input here.'

Sofia looked between Alessandro and Amelia, and it

was only because a part of him was trained almost exclusively on Amelia at all times that he noticed an imperceptible nod from Amelia that seemed to give Sofia some kind of reassurance.

Warning bells sounded in his mind, loud and impossible to ignore. Something was going on. He didn't know what yet, and he couldn't work out why, but he didn't like it at all. So while he gave Sofia the pitch he knew by heart, his mind tried to calculate all possible angles that could be played here. But he kept running up against one.

Amelia. If anyone needed this deal to go ahead as much as he did, it was her. He couldn't see what was in it for her to sabotage this.

'What happened to the original partner?'

'It was discovered that they didn't have the capability to see the project through,' he replied, holding Sofia's enigmatic gaze.

Obeid raised the wing of a midnight-black eyebrow in surprise. 'That is either incompetent or inept.'

Alessandro kept his mouth shut, refusing to dignify her statement with a response.

'I heard you were hours away from signing,' she pressed again.

'We were,' he admitted. 'But I'm not the only one at this table who has backed out of their obligations at the last minute,' he said, his tone cracked like a whip, lashing out at yet another betrayal.

Obeid simply held his gaze. A lesser person might

have flinched. Instead, what he read in Sofia's blue-black eyes was only impatience. As if she'd been surprised it had taken them this long to get to this part of the conversation.

'Good. We are done playing polite, then?' she asked, her cut-glass tone unflinching.

In the corner of his eye, he saw that Amelia looked away from the table.

'I don't believe you would have ever approached me unless you had absolutely no other option.'

'This is true,' he replied, his tone level now that hostilities were almost open on the table. 'But that doesn't mean I don't have a choice.'

'Explain.'

His stomach ground down at the thought of it, but he knew that Gianni would agree with him. They had lived too long with someone else's foot on their necks to ever allow themselves, or Rossi Industries, to be in that same position again.

'My choice. Partner with you, or drop the project altogether.'

But they would lose millions, a voice screamed in Amelia's head. *Not to mention the damage done to their reputation.*

No, no, no, no, no. Her pulse fluttered at a frantic speed and she looked to Sofia, who was considering Alessandro's words.

'And the money you have already invested in the

project? Not to mention the irrevocable damage to your illustrious reputation?'

'Are nothing in comparison to our integrity,' Alessandro replied resolutely. Something twisted in her heart. This was the Alessandro that she had been with in Hong Kong. Integrity, loyalty, pride. She'd been confused by it, torn between the belief that he was corrupt and the instinctive knowledge that he wasn't. Amelia drew in a shaky breath and held it, appreciating the significance his words would have for Sofia.

'I know something of that, Mr Rossi,' Sofia replied. 'Some reputations are earned, some are not. Some are fabricated by bitterness, jealousy and lies and some are simply misunderstandings. If you want to move ahead as partners, I would like that.' She caught a flash of surprise in the tightening across Alessandro's shoulders, but his face betrayed nothing. 'My assistant has sent Ms Seymore several direct references of previous partnerships who are happy to speak to you plainly and truthfully about their experience working with my company.'

Sofia rose from the table, and though Alessandro rose to bid her farewell, he stayed at the table as Amelia walked her from the villa.

It was just the shade of the interior that broke a cool sweat between her shoulder blades, Amelia told herself. The meeting was a success, she had to hold onto that.

Sofia turned just before reaching the front door. 'He knows,' the other woman warned her.

Amelia nodded. 'I know,' she replied, heart see-sawing painfully. She'd known the risk before arranging the meeting. 'He's not stupid.'

Something close to sympathy shone in Sofia's gaze. 'This is a dangerous game, Lia. I hope you know what you're doing.'

Amelia nodded, the warning an echo of the one Alessandro had given her only days earlier. But neither had recognised that the game had already been played and lost, she and Alessandro just hadn't admitted it yet.

She closed the door behind a woman who had once been her closest school friend ten years ago, and turned to find Alessandro staring at her from the end of the hallway, anger, bitterness and something else in his gaze that was quickly eaten up by the darkness.

'You are right about one thing. I'm not stupid,' he said, before turning on his heel and disappearing. And her heart dropped.

Despite that, she raced after him, desperate to explain before any more damage could be done. She reached the courtyard to find him pacing back and forth, all of the emotions he'd kept contained during the meeting finally unleashed in movement that reminded her of a caged panther.

'Alessandro—'

'But I am though, aren't I?' he demanded, his nostrils flaring at deep, quick breaths heaving his chest.

'Are what?'

'A fool!' he roared. 'A fool you have played not once,

but twice. *Cristo.*' He cradled his head in his hands. 'How could I have ever trusted you?'

His words stung like a whip against her back. 'You can't, and you won't. Which is why it didn't matter,' she said, the truth almost too painful to bare.

Her response jerked his head from his hands. 'It didn't matter?' he demanded.

'No. All that mattered was that the meeting was a success. Sofia is—*was*—an old friend. We lost touch after I was forced to change schools. When I realised I needed to fix the Firstview problem, I reached out to her. She's been mistreated badly by…well. That's her story to tell. Safe to say, her reputation is unjust. Her only condition to meeting with a rich, Italian business titan who would never have considered lowering himself to meet with an Arabic businesswoman with a bad reputation was that I keep my existing relationship with her a secret.'

Her words were like barbs and she could see that they had struck home. Amelia knew what it was like to have to prove herself in a male-dominated world, and she couldn't even begin to imagine how hard it must be for Sofia. The dark shadows in her old friend's eyes were enough broad strokes to suggest that her road had been a hard one. But Amelia wouldn't let Alessandro throw this deal away because he was too stubborn to see the wondrous possibility of its success.

'That is unfair,' he said of her last words.

'But true. You are not the only one who has something at stake with this deal. This will be the making of her company—a chance to rise above rumour and prejudice. You will get to move ahead and achieve the success you forecasted for this project.

'And what will you get?' he demanded, the expectation of her betrayal vibrant in his gaze.

She could lie to him, but Amelia was so tired, and, unable to fight it any more, she confessed the truth. 'More. I'd wanted more between us.'

CHAPTER NINE

MORE? HIS INTERNAL voice roared. *She wanted more?*

'By lying?' he demanded incredulously.

'You can't have it both ways, Alessandro,' she replied. 'I undid the damage that I had done with the First-view deal. You didn't set rules as to how I did it.' She looked up at him, her eyes wide with stubborn-willed refusal to back down. 'And it wasn't a lie,' she ground out through clenched teeth.

She was a magnificent madness in his veins. They stood, toe to toe, breathing heavy and hard and hot and all he could think of was how much he wanted to take her mouth with his, to plunder the complex essence of Amelia Seymore.

'I have done all that I can do,' she said. 'The decision is now yours.'

For a moment, he wasn't sure whether she was talking about the deal or the unspoken thing that practically throbbed in the air between them. Anger, resentment, need and want thrashed in his chest, twisting and turning, desperate to get out.

As if she sensed it, her pupils flared beneath the heat of his attention, the flutter in her neck flickering in a way that made him want to see if he could feel it beneath the pad of his thumb. Feel that she was as affected as him, know the truth of it in her body—a body that couldn't lie or betray him.

He forced himself to turn away and missed the flash of hurt that throbbed in Amelia's eyes.

You can't, and you won't. Which is why it didn't matter.

Her words taunted him as he stalked from the villa. Because she was right. He couldn't trust her, wouldn't. He punched Gianni's number into his phone, unsurprised but annoyed when he was told that it was still out of reach.

At the very least, he should have felt satisfied. With Obeid the project could go ahead if he and Gianni wanted it to. He should have felt relief, he should have felt victorious. So why was guilt slashing wounds into his chest at the memory of Amelia's words, of her accusation that he'd never trust her?

Because you want to.

The startling realisation pulled him up short.

He wanted to believe her, just as he'd wanted to believe his mother when she'd promised she'd take them away from his father and uncle.

And he'd never wanted anything more in his entire life. His father and uncle had become so much worse after their mother passed away that they had driven Gianni's mother from the house leaving Gianni behind. Alessandro's mother was all they'd had left but when Saverio had come in from the fields there was only so much Alessandro had been able to do to distract his father from his anger towards his mother. His desperation had been almost suffocating as he'd pleaded with her to take them away after one particularly brutal night.

We'll leave. I'll come for you and we'll leave.

Gianni and he had stayed up all night, whispering reassurances and making plans through the minutes and hours, neither wanting to give up hope that Aurora Vizzini would come to take them away. Even as dawn had crested over the vineyards, and they'd rubbed sleep and sadness from their eyes, knowing that Alessandro's mother had lied, the worst of it had been the hope; the desperate hope he'd had, the need to believe his mother when she had said that she would take them away, that they would be safe.

Nothing was spoken about that night ever again, not with his mother and not with Gianni. And sometimes, in the dead of night, he drove himself to distraction wondering if his mother's promise had even happened.

But Amelia was different, an inner voice taunted him. Her first concern, when he'd brought her to Italy, was her sister. The protective instinct and determination in her so clear and obvious he almost couldn't believe it. Truth had been the only note he'd heard when she'd told him of her childhood. And he'd read between the lines to see deeper, to *know* that she would do anything to protect her family. That she had sacrificed for her family, for what she thought was right. And she'd done it again when she'd agreed to lie to him for Obeid, putting Rossi Industries above her own needs, above *him*. Because she had known what that concealment would do to him.

But that anger—that constant simmering presence beneath his surface whenever she was near—lashed out. So much his life had changed in the space of just days. Or, he wondered, had the change started all those weeks ago in Hong Kong? When success, respect and admiration had led them down a path he'd never thought he'd take? One wrong move had completely undone the entire chessboard of his life. A move he was fighting hard not to repeat.

I'd wanted more between us.

The decision is now yours.

His mind hurt from working out all the angles, exhausted from days of too little sleep and entirely too much adrenaline. It had weakened his resolve and all he wanted, all he needed, was a taste of her to quench the maddening thirst for her.

He looked up to find himself back at the villa, his steps unconsciously bringing him back to where he needed to be. He found Amelia pacing in the living area.

Worry had etched lines across her features, a few wisps of hair had loosened from where it had been pinned back, but shutters came down on her concern as she turned to stand tall and proud beneath the storm of his gaze, determined to meet him head-on. No. Amelia Seymore might have lost her battle, but she wouldn't let herself be cowed.

And he hated how much that turned him on. He'd thought he'd recognised it, the fight. He'd thought that was what fed the burning lava hot in his veins, he'd thought anger was what had locked his chest in a vice ever since he'd left her at the villa hours before. He'd thought fury was what had driven him here.

But he'd been wrong.

In that one moment, he realised that it wasn't she who had fooled him. No. He had fooled *himself.* Because the only thing that was riding him now, and riding him hard, was the sheer desperation to feel her touch, to taste her once again, to feel her wrapped around him as she screamed his name.

He closed the distance between them in two short strides, gathering her into his arms, and claimed her mouth with an undeniable and unyielding possession. A gasp that sounded like surrender and felt like fire engulfed his soul. *Mine.* And in a single heartbeat, her name etched itself irrevocably deep within him.

Every single defence she'd thought she had against him crumbled the moment his lips met hers. A summer storm, fierce and furious, answering every single one of her unspoken prayers—and then as quickly as he had come for her, he tore his mouth from hers.

'*Cristo,*' he said, his forehead pressed against hers,

his chest heaving with their shared breath. 'Please,' he all but begged, 'send me away. Tell me you don't want this.'

'I can't,' she replied, closing her eyes against the sheer intensity of all that she wanted and all that she feared she would never have. But she wouldn't, couldn't hide from this any more. Opening her eyes, she looked deep into his gaze, saw the storm that threatened on the horizon and faced it. 'Because I do want this.'

'Then we're both damned.'

He claimed her lips with such possession for a moment she lost herself. She was his creature—one of pure sensation, responding only to his touch, his taste. The tongue taking her mouth teased her heart, the hands pulling her to him left fingerprints on her soul. And for the briefest moments she surrendered to it, luxuriating in the shocking intensity of his desire, before her own became too much to ignore.

Leaning into his kiss, her hands flew to his chest, fingers fisting the superfine cotton of his shirt and pulling him into her, deepening a kiss she'd already opened herself up to. She felt as much as heard the growl build from Alessandro, raising the hairs at her nape not from fear of him, but fear that she might not be rid of this feeling, this sensual high that fizzed and popped and burst through her body. She wanted to call it madness, but beneath it, beneath the intoxicating fever of his touch, it was the sanest she'd felt since Hong Kong. Because while her heartbeat raged out of control, he soothed her soul.

'Amelia.' He said her name like a plea—as if he too had finally found that same sense of peace. But as he pulled away from her, she followed him, unwilling—unable—to break the connection. Her lips found his and he groaned into the kiss in a way that melted her body against him.

Rising to her tiptoes, she pressed herself to the length of his body, desperate to feel the steely outline of toned and taut male heat against her. Heat flashed over her from the evidence of his arousal, coalescing deep in her throbbing sex.

Despite the ferocity of his kiss, he was being gentle with her, his touches light, his hold careful and it only frustrated her, making her want more. Because she knew what it was like when Alessandro Rossi lost himself in his desire and that, *that*, was what had kept her heart racing when she'd known he was near, *that* was what had filled her dreams with such eroticism she'd ached when awake. *That* was what she wanted now.

Reluctantly she pulled back from the kiss, studying the scorching heat of his gaze—a heat wrapped in chains. He wanted this as much as she did but he was holding himself back. She could almost read the thoughts in his eyes, the warring conflict of should they, shouldn't they.

The words she'd said to Alessandro that night in Hong Kong rose to her lips, a symmetry and irony to it that made her heart hurt a little.

'Just tonight. Just now. But we will never speak of it. Ever.'

Before she'd even finished the sentence, Alessandro had closed the distance between them, crowding her body in the most delicious of ways.

'Amelia, what we do now, here? We *will* speak of it.' The authority in his tone sent shivers of arousal across her skin, tightening her nipples, throbbing between her legs. 'We will acknowledge it. It will not be ignored. Not again. Do you understand?'

The sting of his admonishment dissolved beneath a tide of need so acute, so powerful, she trembled. The pure possession in his gaze, his refusal to ignore this thing between them…it was everything she'd ever wanted.

'Do you want this?' he demanded, and she saw chains holding his desire back begin to snap beneath the heat of their mutual need. She knew what he was asking, knew that it was about more than this one moment, than this night…it was more than the question he'd asked only moments ago.

'Yes. I do,' she replied as he searched her gaze and she opened herself to him, hoping that he saw the truth of her words, of her heart. 'But I want *you*. Not some careful, half touch. So I'm asking, do *you* want this?'

Surprise flared in the rich depths of his gaze. As if he'd thought he'd hidden his feelings better. And she was relieved when he didn't simply dismiss her question, but considered it as seriously as she had. This was the line they would draw—before and after. She knew it as she knew her next breath. And it had to be crossed now or never.

'Yes, I do,' he replied, the last chain of his restraint breaking in his gaze.

Relief sagged through her, but she had no time to dwell on it because that touch that had been gentle was suddenly a brand against her skin. He gathered her in his arms, lifting her up against him. Instinctively she wrapped her legs around his hips so as not to fall—not that she would have. The moment she was in his arms she felt safer than she could ever remember.

He kissed her as he walked them from the living room, the erotic play of his tongue against hers a promise of what was to come when they reached their destination. The arm braced beneath her thighs a tease of where she wanted him to touch her. Her breath caught in her lungs as his other hand wrapped around her hair and gently angled her head back to give him access to her neck as he pressed open-mouthed kisses across her collarbone and down between the v of her breasts, through the oyster satin of her shirt.

Her taut nipples punched at the silk and he covered them with the damp heat of his mouth. Her head fell back on its own, pleasure bursting through her as he reached the bed and laid her gently down on it.

The afternoon had given way to dusk, and still the soft honeyed rays of the sun streamed through white linen curtains. It was the exact opposite to Hong Kong and Alessandro was glad. He refused to allow this moment to be shrouded in darkness or secrecy. He wanted the light, wanted reality; undeniable, unhidden reality.

He wanted to see every single inch of her as he brought her to climax, he wanted to feel it and know it was real. A blush rose to Amelia's cheeks in response to the thoughts she could read in his gaze, he realised. And he bared himself and his desires to her as he reached up to undo the buttons on his shirt one by one.

She bit her lips, watching his hands lower down his body, hungry and heavy. Without taking her eyes from him, she reached behind her to undo one of those tantalising little buttons and drew the shirt over her head. He had reached the last of his shirt buttons as she did so. They both discarded their tops at the same time, eyes for nothing but each other.

He stood, frozen still at the sight of her lace-covered breasts, and when she leaned back on her elbows, his arousal shoved painfully against his trousers. The look in her eyes was pure want. His mouth ran dry and, spellbound, he climbed onto the bed, unable to resist the lure of her.

Instinct took over, powerful and primal and intense. He gently tugged at her ankle, pulling her down the bed as he rose to meet her, covering her body with his, and the sigh he bit back turned into a groan of sheer desire. He slipped an arm beneath her, gathering her to him as he feasted on the smooth planes of her chest and the wide v between her perfect breasts. With one hand he pulled at the lace cup of her bra, exposing her nipple, taut and tempting. He took her breast into his mouth, gorging on pleasure and teasing cries of delight from Amelia.

Her hands flew to his head, fisting in his hair, pulling, pushing as if she wasn't sure whether she wanted more or less of the delicious torment. 'Alessandro…'

'Tell me what you want, *amato*,' he said, desperate to bring her pleasure. 'Tell me what you want and you shall have it.'

She arched, as he turned his attention to her other breast, tugging the lace down and feasting on her flesh. There hadn't been so many words between them in Hong Kong. The shocking intensity of their passion like a sudden firestorm, burning to extremes before burning out. But here? Now? This would be different. This would be no quick thing, he silently promised them both.

'Your desires are safe with me,' he said, pulling back so that she could see the truth of his words. 'Your needs are safe with me. *You* are safe with me.'

The flare of her pupils reminded him of a solar eclipse. Desire blotting out rationality and restraint. 'Put your hands on me,' she said, her tone husky with arousal and need.

'As you wish.'

He found the fastening of her trousers, flicking the button and making quick work of the zip. She shivered as his palm slipped beneath the cotton fabric and caressed the curve of her backside. She cried out as his fingers delved beneath the lace of her panties into the delicate soft wet heat of her.

In a single breath he was more aroused than he'd

ever been in his life, and even then, holding back from what he wanted was shockingly easy in order to give her more.

He wanted this, her pleasure. He wanted to see starbursts in her eyes, not confusion, doubt or worry. He wanted to see what he had seen in Hong Kong. Feel what he had felt there. A gasp fell from her lips and he wanted to taste it, taste the surrender to all that was passion and sensuality on her lips. His heart pounded against his ribcage as she shifted in his arms, her eyes becoming soft and unfocused as his fingers circled her clitoris, sweeping around the soft delicate flesh and returning again and again to a sensual torment that teased them both in equal measure.

He studied every part of her face, the way that she bit her lower lip trying and failing to contain her responses, responses that were like a drug to him. *He* did this to her, *he* gave her this. A flush stained her cheeks and crept up her neck, her eyes closed then opened, unseeing, lost in sensation and sensual frustration as her orgasm danced just out of her reach.

In seconds, he had pulled at her trousers, slipped them from beneath her and removed them from her legs. Carefully caressing his way back, his hand pressed her thighs apart gently and he lowered himself between her legs. The heat of her gaze on him seared his soul, and as he parted her to him he felt her flinch. 'You are safe with me,' he promised again, as he gave into his need for the most intimate of kisses.

Her learned her song then, the cadence of her pleasure—in the cries and moans and pleas that filled the air. His heartbeat pounded the rhythm, the sound of his blood roaring in his veins the base line, and above it all rose a melody so sweet he'd never tire of hearing it, and when her orgasm crested, the crescendo was so powerful, he felt changed by it.

He gentled her with soft touches and words as she came back down—as affected by her pleasure as she had been. But when her eyes found his, focused, intent and full of need for more, his body answered without a thought.

He kissed her with the desperation of a dying man, as if this were the last thing he would do with his life. His body, hot and feverish for her touch, relished the way her hands skated across his skin, fingers soothing and then gripping his shoulders, biceps, flanks—as if she wanted to explore every inch of him.

Alessandro pulled away reluctantly to remove his trousers, his gaze not leaving hers once. Automatically he reached for his wallet and withdrew a condom from it and stopped to look at it in his hands. His mind utterly blank because…because…she was already pregnant.

Never, not once in his entire life, had he had sex without protection. Never had he been skin to skin with anyone and, looking up, he saw the same thought reflected in Amelia's eyes.

The realisation of how important this moment was nudged its way through the haze of Amelia's climax.

For a man who had sworn never to have children, she imagined the question about whether to use protection or not would be as alien to him as it was to her. But she was pregnant already and the desire to feel him—to be with him—without a barrier between them suddenly became more than just a want. It was a need that she couldn't explain. Carefully she reached out to take the condom from his fingers and placed it on the side table.

He looked at her, studying her intently, and she opened herself up to him—laying herself bare to his silent inquisition. She wanted this and she trusted him. And in that moment, she saw that trust reflected back at her.

The bonds holding Alessandro back shattered and her heart soared to see the ferocious desire riding her hard reflected in his gaze. He leaned across the bed and thrust her into a realm of infinite pleasure with his kiss, the press of his body against hers igniting a hunger she feared would never be sated.

She wrapped her arms around him and held on tight, half afraid that he'd leave, as if already she could feel him slipping through her fingers. But the thought disappeared as he bent his head to her chest and claimed her breast as if it were already his.

Pleasure arrowed through her to the heart of her sex and when his deft fingers gently pressed her legs apart and delved into that exact same place, she couldn't contain the cry of sheer want that left her lips.

He gently pushed her legs aside to make space for

himself and she trembled when she felt the jut of his erection against her sex. Both Amelia's and Alessandro's eyes drifted shut from the shared pleasure of the moment, luxuriating in the sensations that were new to them both, until neither could resist the lure of what was to come.

Slowly, Alessandro pushed into her, her muscles tightening, flexing, drawing him further into her. Amelia tried to capture the feeling with words, but nothing stuck, flitting away on a tide of sheer sensation and connection. They were both trembling with the force of their pleasure, with the shock of it, the surprise. It twisted something deep in Amelia, turned it, opening it into something beautiful. He filled her so perfectly that she felt as if they had been made for each other, as if finally something was beginning to make sense for her and her journey.

And then, when she thought she couldn't take any more feeling, he began to withdraw and she cried out at the loss. A rueful smile pulled at Alessandro's lips and in Italian he rained down praises and promises as he pushed into her again, and again, and again. The erotically slow strokes he teased them with seemed endless to her, launching her into that strange infinite place, until it seemed even Alessandro Rossi couldn't take it any more.

As his movements became quicker, his thrusts more powerful, their connection became more tangible. Sweat beaded his brow, her neck, between her shoulder blades, and down his chest, the air became hot with cries and moans and pants and pleas.

Harder and harder and higher and higher he drove her to the pinnacle of her climax until finally, just when she thought she couldn't take any more, Alessandro thrust them over the edge into an abyss of nothing but sheer pleasure.

CHAPTER TEN

It took a while for Amelia to realise she wasn't asleep any more. Nestled into the curve of Alessandro's huge frame, with his arm clamped over her waist, it had felt like an impossible dream. In Hong Kong, she'd not allowed herself to sleep. She'd stolen from the hotel room while Alessandro had been in the bathroom, unable to face the consequences of her actions…until those consequences had come looking for her.

But here, there was no chance of her sneaking out of bed. Alessandro's arm was a weight holding her in place and he, apparently, slept like the dead. It was such a normal everyday thing to know about him that it made her smile, and burrow deeper into his embrace, close her eyes and fall back asleep.

When Amelia woke, she was alone. The heat, the safety, the promise of the night before—noticeably absent. Alessandro was in the bathroom and she wondered if she'd conjured the comparison with Hong Kong into reality. Should she leave? Should she stay? Would he emerge from the bathroom with a smile, a frown, or that purposefully blank look that meant he was waiting to take his lead from her?

This was the father of her child and she didn't know. Hurt swirled with guilt. It wasn't good enough. She had to do better, *they* had to do better. Now that her sabotage had been undone, she had to turn her attention to them. Because if she did want the security he offered and the relationship her child deserved, then she had to feel more than…than…discomfort and awkwardness. She looked at her ringless finger and wondered if perhaps it might for ever be bare now. A ring promising her to Alessandro far too much to ever dream of, let alone hope for.

I want a chance.

She knew that Alessandro would keep their agreement, but it was what she did with that chance that mattered now. For the sake of their child, they needed to get to know each other, outside the boardroom and the bedroom. She just had to figure out how.

She slipped from the silken sheets of his bed, returned to her room, and took a shower, thinking about how she could achieve what she wanted. She rolled her shoulders beneath the spray of the powerful jets and felt his palm trace the length of her spine. She soaped her skin and felt his open-mouthed kisses and the pleasant ache between her thighs from where she had gripped him, urged him, held him deep within her. But despite the pleasure he had given her last night, the satisfaction, her body craved him again. It was a drumbeat just be-

neath her skin, always, constant, somehow slipping into
time with her pulse. Reluctantly she pulled her thoughts
back to the idea beginning to form in her mind. It was a
little…*simple* but she believed that it would be effective.

By the time Alessandro emerged from the hotel suite
room Amelia had dismissed the staff to give them some
privacy, and was waiting for him at the table. He was
dressed as if ready for the office, as always, and still as
desperately handsome as he had been the night before.
Any hope that their shared passion might have somehow taken the edge off her desire for him was dashed,
instantly and irrevocably.

His gaze flickered from her to the table and confusion pulled at his brow. He was probably wondering why
there were bits of torn paper in a glass jar. She nudged
the steaming shot of espresso she had made him and
steeled herself. She was about to explain when—

'I've offered Obeid the Aurora project and she has
agreed.'

Amelia's mouth shut with a snap. It was as she'd
expected, but she couldn't help but feel hurt at being
excluded.

'The team in London will push on with it from here.'

She stiffened, realising the implications of his words.

*What did you think would happen, Amelia? That he'd
keep you on the project?*

'You will no longer—'

'I understand,' she interrupted him, curt in her desire
to not hear him say it. For two years working for Ales-

sandro had been a ruse. But it also hadn't been. She'd enjoyed the work she'd done there. She'd been good at it too. But right now? She had more important things to worry about.

He studied her acceptance with something like scepticism that only proved her point.

'Will you sit?' she asked, pushing aside the small bruise forming on her heart.

'We should be getting back to the jet.'

She clenched her teeth together, fighting the impulse to reveal just how affected she was by his dismissal. He might be the boss, but he seemed to have forgotten that she had never been a mere underling who jumped at his every whim. He caught her gaze, held it, testing the strength of her will and, clearly finding it unbending, he took the chair opposite her.

There was an air of impatience about him and it was this, this power struggle, this discord that they had to get over.

'I am pregnant,' she stated.

'*Sì?*' he replied, his confusion evident.

'The threat hanging over the Aurora project and Rossi Industries has been neutralised.'

Begrudgingly, it seemed, he acknowledged that statement with a curt nod. '*Sì.*'

'But you don't trust me. You want me. I know that,' she said, a blush rising to her cheeks as she maintained control of the conversation. 'But you don't, we don't... *know* each other.'

His gaze flickered to the jar on the table that contained lots of little folds of paper.

'Yet,' she hurried to clarify. 'We don't know each other yet.' Amelia took a breath. 'You've said that you will protect our child financially and, I'm sure, well beyond that. But our child will need more than just financial support and physical security.'

It was something that she had learned the moment that both those things had been ripped away from her and her sister. Using that memory to give her strength, she asked, 'What about their emotional needs? In those precious first few months and years, and then later on in life? And where will we live? Will we even live together?' she asked, seeing his eyes flare in response to her last question. 'I want…to do this *with* you. I don't want to tell you about my first scan after the fact, or first steps or first anything. I want you to be there with us, I want… I want to share it with you.'

And it wasn't just for her child, Amelia realised as her heart quivered in her chest, waiting for his response. For years she had taken the reins, looked after her sister, taken care of her mother, made the hard decisions and had the difficult arguments and still, despite that, she wanted to give him part of this and it terrified her. Because if she learned to rely on him, if she learned to lean on him and he walked away? It would break her heart permanently.

But she couldn't let fear deter her and she pressed on. 'I don't know how long Issy and Gianni will be away, but when my sister comes back, I want to share this news with the happiness that it deserves. I want to be able to tell her what my future and our child's future is going to look like in the next few months. There is nothing that can be done about the Aurora project now for at least another week. And I want... I'm *hoping* that you will give us that time for us to learn enough about each other to see if this might work? To see if we can be more. To see if...you can trust me.'

Alessandro couldn't pretend that he hadn't seen the sincerity and the need behind her questions. She had laid herself more open here than in what they had shared last night. And her hopes fed almost directly into his daydreams, fantasies that were becoming more like wishes with each moment he shared with her. Wishes that had gold bands and diamond rings that shocked as much as scared him.

But he couldn't pretend that he didn't feel a sense of panic, a sense of being rushed that made him anxious, as if his hand was being forced before he'd had time to think things through properly himself.

He thought about what she'd said about Gianni and her sister. The moment he'd finished his call with Sofia he'd sent word to St Lovells, ensuring that his cousin would at least know that the project had been saved and there was now no longer any threat to Rossi Industries. But hadn't he avoided speaking directly to Gianni because he had no idea how to explain to the man closer to him than any brother what was happening with Amelia?

No matter what he felt, though, the last thing he would allow was for his child to grow up amongst frigid cordiality or burning mistrust and resentment. He and Amelia *did* need to work together to find a way through it all for the sake of their child.

'What are you suggesting?' he asked, curious as to how what she was hoping for fitted into the folded pieces of paper in the jar.

'I have written out a number of things we can do together.'

Dios mio. 'Amelia. Is this the romantic version of team-building exercises?'

He instantly wished he could call the errant thought back, until Amelia's surprised laugh fell between them, lightening the mood and brightening her eyes in the most incredible way. 'It is the solution to a problem,' she forced out through her smile.

Reluctant to lose the moment, he eyed the folded paper suspiciously and continued to play the grouch. 'Fine, but if you expect me to fall back with my eyes closed and trust that you'll catch me—'

This time the laughter that erupted from Amelia was fresh and wild like the flowers on the meadow between his and Gianni's estates.

'You'd crush me,' she replied, after successfully swallowing her laugh.

He couldn't help the responding pull at the corner of his lips, or the way that it captured Amelia's gaze.

'I would,' he agreed and, somehow, they were no longer talking about trust exercises. Shaking the erotic thoughts from his increasingly dirty mind, he took a sip of the espresso, only mildly cooler since it had been made. She knew how he liked his coffee. Black and scalding. He refused to acknowledge it, but it meant something to him. 'Okay,' he said, taking a deep breath. 'But,' he said, bargaining, 'I reserve the right to veto.'

She considered his offer. 'You can have *one*,' she countered.

He narrowed his eyes, assessing her as an opposing player in this game she had created.

'If I do this, then you will do the same ones that I pick,' he demanded.

This time she narrowed her eyes as—he imagined— she remembered whatever it was she had written on those little pieces of paper. He held his breath, despite believing that she wouldn't have asked him to do any-thing that she wouldn't do herself.

'Okay,' she agreed.

Something eased in his chest. 'Then let's play,' he said, reaching towards the jar.

Amelia's hand shot out to halt him, drawing his eyes to hers. He would feel the punch to his gut for days.

'It's not a game,' she said quietly.

He just about managed to stop the flinch that pulled at his body. She was right and he knew it. There needed to be trust. They needed to find some kind of accord, because he couldn't, wouldn't let his child grow up in an environment that remotely resembled the one he had been born into. He would make sure that their child had better.

'I know, Amelia,' he promised.

You are safe with me.

His words from last night echoed into his mind, his vow one that he had meant and one that he wouldn't break.

'So, I just…' He dipped his hand into the jar and riffled around inside as he'd seen children do at the local village fete his father and uncle had tried to sell their horrible wine at.

The thanks in her eyes was painful to bear—that it was for such a small thing. Had he really been acting like such a monster? Swallowing, he pulled out a tear of paper and unfolded it. There in looping handwriting that belonged to Amelia was not what he had expected to read. He had been prepared for a checklist—dinner out, a film maybe. Even an art gallery.

He should have known better.

'Are they all like this?'

She nodded, watching him carefully.

'And you will also do these?' he reminded her.

'I will do every one that you do,' she said.

He placed the piece of torn paper on the table, smoothing it flat with his fingers as if the sudden slap of pain raised by this simple request hadn't caught him by surprise.

Take me somewhere from your childhood.

He cleared his throat. *Cristo.*

'Veto,' he said, not caring what weakness it revealed in him. He would never take her anywhere near his childhood. She nodded, looking sad but not surprised. Instead, she passed him the jar. He pulled another tear of paper, trying hard not to tense up from fear of what this one might say, and opened it.

Show me something you're proud of.

And he soon realised just how clever she really was. There was no doubt that after even just a few of these that sense of connection he'd felt from the very first would be strengthened. At least, he could readily acknowledge, his child would have a mother who would fight for them and fight hard, no matter the cost.

'Okay,' he said, sliding back his chair. 'Let's go.'

Amelia was only a little surprised to be heading back to Italy. Part of her had imagined that they would be on their way to London, to The Ruby that was the heart of his and Gianni's company or any of the other incredible buildings Rossi Industries had developed across the globe. But instead, they touched down at the same private airfield they had left the day before, the relatively short flight time between Italy and Morocco still a wonder to her.

Alessandro had been tight-lipped from the moment

that he unfolded the first piece of paper. She'd caught sight of the one he'd vetoed and, although she understood why, it had still hurt to be shut out from such a huge part of what made him *him*.

And she was *so* drawn to him, she forced herself to acknowledge now. Handsome, powerful, brooding, absolutely and unquestionably. But it was the flashes of fallibility that sank claws into her, the lightness that he kept well hidden beneath that serious exterior—the way that, despite all his authority and power, he could still get flustered by her, that he could still be amusingly petulant. Beneath all the layers of hurt and damage done by his parents and her father, she could see glimpses of the boy he might have been and she grieved the loss of that boy with such intensity it shocked her to the core.

Amelia could understand the damage, hurt and fear that had led Alessandro to make that promise years ago. But in denying himself a future family, someone to love and be loved by, he had shrunk the people around him to one or two and she wanted more—not for her child and herself, but *him*. She wanted more for Alessandro than what he had allowed himself.

Rather than the sleek black car she expected, a small Prussian blue old MG convertible two-seater sparkled in the sunlight on the runway. She frowned and cast her gaze back to the staff carrying their luggage.

'Don't worry, *tesoro*. Our belongings will be taken back to the villa. We're just taking a detour along the way.'

The term of endearment was almost carelessly

thrown her way, as if it hadn't been one of the words
he'd whispered over and over and over again to her last
night as they'd made love. She wouldn't, couldn't regret it. It had been the most magical experience of her
life so far, but she knew that it would make it so much
more difficult if this plan—the plan for her child's future happiness—went awry.

He opened the door for her, his chivalry ingrained
in a way that felt natural and touching.

'Where are we going?' she couldn't help but ask.

'You'll see. For now, just enjoy the ride,' he said,
slipping his sunglasses on, putting the car into gear and
letting the engine loose in a roar that sent vibrations
through her body. She laughed and the smile across
Alessandro's features took another bite out of her heart.

An hour later, they pulled up to a residential street
on the outskirts of a small town. It was pretty, but she
wasn't quite sure what made it so particular to the billionaire beside her. He parked in a bay and got out of
the car and, leaning against the silken surface, looked
at a building on the opposite side of the road. It was
the Italian equivalent of a two-up, two-down, Amelia
thought as she realised that this was what he wanted to
show her. A family came out of the door, the parents too
distracted by their children to notice them by the car.
Risking a glance at Alessandro, she saw a small smile
pull at the corner of his lips as if happy to see the ram-
bunctious family spilling from the house.

'When we realised we couldn't build on the land your

father sold us, we were in trouble.' He shook his head, and cleared his throat. He didn't need to explain—she'd seen the terrible terms of the loan he and Gianni had taken to buy the land from her father, she knew how urgent the repayment schedule had been.

'We had to do something else and quickly. Renovating and reselling was our best option, so we started with this one. This house. We worked day and night, just the two of us, grit, determination, and a hell of a lot of luck. So many things could have gone wrong. But we did it. Renovated, decorated, sold and bought. We did it over and over and over again, flipping houses until we had enough capital to pay back the loan and start developing our own property. But this? This was the first house. This was the one that started what would one day be Rossi Industries.

'It's humble and I'm okay with that. But what I'm really proud of? Was that we got back up. We didn't let it break us. We got back up and we kept going, kept moving forward.'

His gaze, hidden behind his sunglasses, would have been full of vehemence but she didn't need to see it to feel it. She knew that need. That driving force pushing you back up, pushing you on, unable to break no matter what was thrown at you. Because he'd had Gianni and she'd had Issy and another thread was woven in place, binding them together, even if it was against their own will.

'Your turn,' Alessandro said, twisting the conversation away from himself and his past.

Amelia glanced at the café at the end of the road and he levered himself away from the car, offering his arm in a gesture that was supposed to be ironic, but, when she slipped her hand through the crook of his arm, was anything but.

When they sat at a table on the pavement shown to them by a waiter who barely spared them a glance he smiled, realising that he missed this. The simplicity of having a coffee and not needing to rush because of a meeting, or decision or...

Amelia was looking at him. He felt her gaze like a touch, a caress. Softer than he probably deserved and hotter than he expected. But when he caught it, and held it, a blush rose to her cheeks and memories of the night before crashed through his mind.

The waiter slapped down a bottle of water and impatiently demanded their orders. Amelia hid the choke of a laugh behind her hand as Alessandro ordered them coffee and a selection of pastries, sure that Amelia would be hungry by now.

'That's funny to you? People being rude to me?' he asked, amused by her reaction.

'I just wondered what your staff would think to have seen that interaction.'

'Why?'

'Well, they are...in awe of you. I doubt they'd even believe their eyes.'

He frowned. 'I don't...am I...?' He rarely stuttered, but the thought that his staff might be in any way intimidated by him was terrible.

As if sensing his thoughts, she reached across the table, her small fine hands cool despite the heat. 'No. You are an excellent boss. You can just be a little *stern*.'

He nodded, acknowledging the truth of it. He knew that. Stern was probably a good description. And when the waiter returned with their drinks and the pastries, he felt the shift in mood, as if she was gearing herself up to meet her part of the task she had set them.

She retrieved her phone, unlocked the screen and swiped it a few times as if searching for something on it. Then she passed it across the table to him where he saw a picture of Amelia with her arm around a beaming brunette, younger than her, but the connection between them unmistakable. Isabelle Seymore was holding a giant ice-cream sundae, the sisters cheek to cheek, the pure joy emanating from them infectious.

'Your sister?'

'Yes,' she said, smiling with such affection it was a physical presence. 'Taken on her eighteenth birthday.'

He frowned, searching Isabelle's features for the differences time had wrought between then and the recent picture of her with Gianni.

'I thought she was blonde.'

'Gianni doesn't like brunettes,' Amelia explained.

It was true. Gianni's tastes ran to blonde, tall, easy and quick—to leave, that was. But instinctively he knew that none of those descriptions would fit Isabelle Seymore.

'This is what you're most proud of?' he asked, distracted as to what her meaning was. Getting her sister to lure his cousin into a trap? Their plans for vengeance?

'My *sister*.' Amelia stressed the words as if reading his thoughts. 'My sister is what I'm most proud of. We weren't always close, not when we were younger.' She smiled ruefully. 'I'd imagine from the outside looking in, we were just two more rich girls spoiled silly for their entire lives. We bickered over unimportant things as if it were the end of the world and took everything, especially each other, for granted. But after... There were so many ways in which Issy could have taken a different path. A darker path. She was younger than me when our father's business collapsed. And in the year that followed both he and our mother battled their own demons. Bit by bit Mum lost herself to addiction and Dad lost his health, as you know.

'But there are so many ways a young woman can hurt without parental stability, so many ways that hurt can be twisted and turned into dangerous things—dangerous self-beliefs... There were so many ways in which she could have fallen off the rails and she didn't.'

'You didn't let her,' he guessed correctly.

'A little. But that doesn't take into account the fact that she is who she is—and that is a genuinely good person. She is an auxiliary nurse on a children's hospital ward. She is *good* in a selfless way that I admire and had absolutely nothing to do with. *She* nurtured that goodness, protected it, not once letting our parents' selfishness darken or break that.'

Just the way she spoke of her sister made him want to meet her. Different from Amelia, because there was a thread of darkness to Amelia. No, not darkness. Just… experience. Acceptance that bad things happened in life, bad things she'd seen and felt. Different from his own, but still present, and fundamentally entwined with him and his.

Because—now that the anger and sense of betrayal over the Aurora deal was dissipating—he could see just how much Amelia had needed to take on at such a young age. To care for her sister, herself and even her mother, that would have been a heavy burden to bear alone, with no real help.

Our only real concern, he remembered one of the senior management members saying of Amelia, *is that her self-sufficiency could lead to an isolation amongst her team members.* At the time, Alessandro hadn't been overly concerned, sure that she was just focusing too much on her projects. But now he wanted to curse the parents who had forced their daughter to grow up far too soon.

He wondered what would have happened to Amelia and her sister if they hadn't been set on the path of revenge that had consumed ten years of their lives. What their lives would have looked like, who they would have been. And then, he couldn't help but wonder what would have happened if Gianni hadn't called him with the news, if he hadn't been warned about Amelia. Not with him, or Rossi Industries, but for the two sisters who would have reached their goal.

'What did you plan to do after?' he asked.

'After?'

'Yes, if you were successful. If you'd brought RI to its knees. What were you going to do after?'

For the first time since he'd known Amelia she looked—blank, desperately trying to hide something behind that nothing expression.

'I don't know,' she whispered, and his heart broke just a little for the girl she had once been.

CHAPTER ELEVEN

AMELIA HAD FELT unsettled ever since the conversation at the café with Alessandro. She couldn't quite put her finger on it, but she couldn't deny that she was feeling out of sorts. Standing in front of the mirror in Alessandro's beautiful en suite in Villa Vittoria, she took in the changes since the day Alessandro found her outside her flat in Brockley.

Despite the subtle sense of unease, her skin was now sun-kissed with a gentle golden glow. Freckles that had only ever shown themselves in Italy had been sprinkled across her forearms and her nose, warming the paler complexion she was used to. Her cheeks, ever so slightly rounder, had taken on an almost permanent blush thanks to the passion that she shared with Alessandro during heady nights she could barely credit were real.

The day after visiting the café, Alessandro had picked another piece of paper from the jar.

Tell me something about yourself that no one else knows.

He could have chosen to speak of so much but secretly she'd been just a little relieved when, instead of delving into the harder conversations available to them, he'd confided that he didn't like cartoons. Obviously, she'd thought he was absurd, but he'd seemed equally bemused when in return she'd shared that she didn't like sandwiches that were cut the wrong way. He'd stared at her for a moment and then made her two sandwiches so that she could illustrate the diagonal cut versus the half cut. He shook his head, threw his hands up in the air and stalked off muttering about silly English sandwiches.

The next morning, Amelia woke to find Alessandro waiting for her with a smile. He held out one of the paper tasks, looking strangely excited.

Take me somewhere you've always wanted to go.

And she'd buried her laughter beneath the sheets because he'd looked so much like an impatient child that she'd half expected to end up in Disneyland. Instead, as the view from the jet's window morphed from stretches of sea into stretches of desert, she realised that they were in Egypt to visit the Pyramids of Giza. None of the pictures she'd seen had done them justice. The sheer size and sense of history was breathtaking, even in spite of the large groups of tourists around them, chatting happily away and taking pictures.

Alessandro had asked if she wanted a private tour,

and she'd declined because she liked the way he was when he was surrounded by people. As if he could relax and disappear in the crowds, rather than adopt that aura of power needed when he was the sole focus. It surprised her how easily he was able to give over that control and that attention and go with the flow of the loud tour guide, and throughout it all she felt his gaze on her almost as much as she saw it on the pyramids.

The following day while making her a decaffeinated coffee, Alessandro asked if there was somewhere she'd always wanted to go. Amelia looked up at him, nestling her cup in the palm of her hand.

'Could we go to Capri?' she asked, yearning in her heart making her pulse a little erratic.

'Of course. If you want, we can take a drive down the Amalfi coast and a boat to cross the gulf of Naples. Or we could take a helicopter if you like?'

She thought back to the last holiday her family had taken together, before her father had given up and before addiction took over her mother. They'd taken a hot, sweaty and *scary* drive down from Naples along the Amalfi coast—her mother hiding her eyes from the oncoming drivers, she and Issy squealing in delight at the twists and turns, too young to know better. It made her smile despite the ache in her heart. 'Boat, I think. I'd really like to take the boat.'

'Are you going to make me stand in line at the ferry terminal with the other tourists?' His demand was full of mock outrage and she was beginning to suspect that he secretly enjoyed being so anonymous.

'Actually, this time I think I'd like it to be just the two of us.'

In what felt like the blink of an eye, Alessandro had whisked them down to Positano and hired the most beautiful little speedboat she'd ever seen. It was like something from an old black and white film. Silken mahogany glowed beneath the Italian sun, perfectly offset by the deep racing green paint, the boat's sleek lines so smooth she wanted to run her hands across it.

Alessandro took the helm with attractive confidence and welcomed her aboard as if she were some grand duchess and he a lowly captain. The playfulness between them was addictive and her heart began to stretch towards the hope that it could always be like this between them.

She closed her eyes, letting the sun's rays warm her, and simply enjoyed the tang of salt in the air, the spray of the water, the rocking of the boat as Alessandro navigated around the deep swells caused by other seafaring craft.

But as they drew closer to the beautiful island, beloved by the rich and famous and lowly tourists alike, a sense of panic began to chip away at her pulse. The waves felt harsh as they jolted her and the grey craggy rocks beneath the lush greenery of the coastline felt threatening. The heat became uncomfortable and she began to feel breathless.

'*Tesoro*, are you okay?'

Usually, the endearment would have warmed her, but it barely even registered as she began to shake her head.

'Is it the baby? Is—?'

'No, it's not the baby. But…can we go back? Can we just…?' She gripped onto the seat beneath her, knuckles white, desperate to hold on while her world swayed in a way that went far beyond the sea.

Her obvious distress caused Alessandro serious concern and he quickly sped them away from the paths of the large tourist ferries and any other vessels, slowing only where it was safe, and he moored them just off a craggy coastal inlet. Turning off the engine, he sat and wordlessly pulled her into his lap, not stopping to question her need for him.

Amelia wrapped her hands around his neck and clung to him as he swept circles on her back, trying to sooth the jagged breaths.

'*Cara…*'

She buried her head in his neck, scared to explain her feelings.

'Whatever it is, Amelia, it will be okay.'

You are safe with me.

Remembered words enticed her to speak, encouraged her to share the feelings so strong they had overwhelmed her.

'How could they?' she whispered. 'How could they have left us like that?' she asked him, even then knowing it was not his place to answer. 'I'm so…angry,' she said, realising the truth of the feeling thundering through her veins. 'I'm furious,' she cried, her hands fisting against the fact that the two people in the world who should have protected her and her sister had been so utterly selfish.

'We lost so much,' she said as the tears dampened Alessandro's linen shirt and her heart buckled beneath the onslaught of her feelings. 'Not money, or houses or friends. We lost *them*.' And for the first time she opened the door to the room where she had locked all that anger and all that resentment—not at having to look after and care for her sister, but resentment of her parents' utter neglect. And as her hurts poured out into the sea around them, Amelia let herself be comforted by the man who had, only days before, been her enemy.

Alessandro whispered to her in Italian; words of comfort to the incredible woman in his arms, until the storm of emotions that had gripped her had passed enough for him to talk to her about it. He knew that fury, he knew how hard it was to keep it controlled—he struggled with that himself. But Amelia, it seemed, had not realised what she had been fighting, her revenge plan keeping her and her sister from realising who had hurt them the most.

In that moment Alessandro wanted to destroy Thomas Seymore all over again. But if he had the chance to do so all over again, would he have? Knowing what it had done to Amelia and Isabelle? He could not take it back, and he could not apologise for it either. It had been a fundamental part of what had made him and Gianni who they were today and he was not, and would not be, ashamed of the men they had become. But that didn't mean he couldn't recognise the damage that had been done to Amelia and Isabelle Seymore's lives by his and Gianni's own need for revenge.

The sigh building deep in his chest was tired and heavy with thoughts of the past, clashing with the hopes he knew Amelia had for the future. A hope to do and be better. And he wanted it. He wanted it so damn much it terrified him. Because he'd had that same look, that same hope, once before and when that hope had been betrayed it had taken him decades to recover. He didn't think he'd survive it again. As if noticing the edge of darkness to his thoughts, Amelia stiffened in his embrace, until he forced the thought from his mind. Determined, instead, to soothe her hurts in this moment.

'Amelia,' he said, pulling back so that she could read the truth of his words. 'I really am truly sorry for what happened to your family. That was never an outcome we intended.'

She nodded her head, but he could still see the upset in her eyes. An almost violent urge to conquer any hurt she faced, any pain, and remove it from her path rocked him to his core. Despite the shocking power of that emotion, he gently swept back a sleek chestnut tendril of hair from her face. 'I'm sorry that you struggled and I'm sorry that you didn't have people there to look after you and take care of you when you needed it most. I'm sorry you had to do so much on your own.'

As he said the words, his own heart turned—like a sunflower following the sun—as if his words were trying to heal a hurt of his own, as if they were just as relevant to his childhood as hers. And this time when tears flowed freely down her cheeks, he knew that they were good tears, healing tears, necessary, so that she could be freer than she had been before. He placed a gentle kiss on a watery smile, and a little laugh escaped her.

'You can't kiss me now, I'm all...gross from crying.'

And Alessandro barked out a laugh. 'Amelia, *cara*, you are many things, but gross is not and never will be one of them.'

'I have a feeling,' she replied ruefully, 'that the next seven months might test that statement.'

For a moment they were caught up in a shared smile, his gaze dropping to her stomach where their child was slowly growing. Amelia, bottom lip pinned by a flash of white teeth, reached for his hand slowly—as if giving him enough time to back away. He felt hypnotised, unable to move—unsure whether he wanted this or not, scared in a way that he only vaguely remembered from a very long time ago. He let her take his hand and she placed it over her abdomen.

Surely, he wouldn't be able to feel the flare of her stomach this early on in the pregnancy, but he imagined that he did. Imagined that in there was the best part of both him and Amelia. They stayed like that for a while, lost in thoughts and hopes and dreams of a future they both wanted too much to say, until the blare of a passenger ferry startled them apart, and they turned to find tourists waving and yelling their greetings across the stretch of water.

Alessandro smiled, to cover the disquiet the moment had brought him, and said instead, 'Shall we go home?'

Amelia would remember the next few days with the hazy glow of summer and heat and a softness that she hadn't encountered before—from Alessandro or anyone other than her sister, for that matter. Alessandro could be funny, she discovered, enjoying the way that she could tease his ego without denting it or provoking a retaliation. He'd made her laugh as he'd answered another paper task to tell her something about Gianni that no one else knew.

She'd not been able to hold back the tears of laughter as Alessandro described in great detail, and a not inconsiderate delight, the time Gianni had tried to 'frost' the tips of his hair with bleach, only to have to shave his head and wait for his hair to grow back.

In exchange she'd told Alessandro about the time that Issy had fallen off her 'Gianni diet', ordered four pizzas, ice cream, garlic bread and sides, then got so scared about what her evil gym instructor would say the next day, she'd been too upset to eat it all, and she'd taken the entire lot downstairs to their neighbour.

Alessandro surprised her again with his impressive

cooking and the fact that he was a secret foodie was almost one of her favourite things about him. From the incredible ingredients in the fully stocked fridge, Alessandro would create dinners at an almost gourmet level. After which, they continued to explore the passion they had discovered in Morocco. Amelia's nights were full of a heady sensuality that left her breathless and wanting in the daylight. Slowly they learned each other's pleasures, indulging in pleasing and receiving in ways that she could never have imagined.

But that, Amelia would later recognise, was the end of that brief momentary paradise they had together. Because the evening they returned from an idyllic day in Umbria, Alessandro received a message from work that had him locked in his office until long past midnight. And when he'd come to their shared bed that night, tiptoeing and trying to be so quiet, she let him think she was still asleep because she didn't have the courage to ask him about it.

The following morning, he was gone from the bed before she woke. But by the time she came down for breakfast, she was surprised to find him waiting for her. When he saw her, he put his phone away and offered her the decaffeinated coffee he had made for her and a slip of torn paper and it didn't matter what the paper said, just that he was still willing to do the silly tasks she had hoped would bring them together.

They were barely twenty minutes' drive away from the estate when he received another call and he cursed.

'You can put it on speaker if you like?' she offered, hoping that way he might be able to continue driving. And maybe, even, that she'd discover what was wrong and see if she could help.

'No, it's okay,' he replied, not meeting her gaze and signalling to pull over.

He got out of the car and took the call, pacing up and down the side of a dusty road. She tried to catch some of the conversation in between the roar from passing cars but it was useless. And she felt…frustrated and cut out. Even if it wasn't the Aurora project, she had worked with him for two years—she was good at her job. She could help if he would let her, but he wouldn't.

'I'm sorry, I have to go back,' he announced when he returned to the car.

The sudden engine ignition and the sweep of the U-turn prevented any further response from her. Only it turned out that Alessandro hadn't meant back to the villa, but back to London. Without her.

He returned that evening and Amelia clung harder to him that night than she had done before, as if sensing that he was slipping through her fingers, just as she had begun to realise that she loved him. It hadn't been quick, or sudden, it hadn't hit her like a punch, or stolen her breath. It had grown, piece by piece, as she'd uncovered little bits of him, like precious stones on a beach, hidden beneath sand and sea.

The loyalty he had to Gianni, the integrity he'd had with his business and his staff, the standard he held himself to, and the drive and determination to succeed. Those had all made him admirable in her mind even as she'd tried to sabotage him. And the physical connection they'd had? The strength of it had overpowered her own mind—her own determination to hate him, to make him pay for what had been done to her family. But his concern and care for her when she had collapsed, and then when she had emotionally broken on the way to Capri, made her feel as if she was seeing the *real* Alessandro Rossi. The way that he made her coffee, made her favourite dishes, those things had built in her heart. He had considered her in a way that no one had ever done before and it made her realise what she would lose if he walked away from her.

She worried about him when he went to London again the next day. The entire time he was away, her focus was on him and what he was doing, what was going wrong to take so much of his focus. And she could hear it, the whispered warning in the back of her mind. That he was cutting her out because he didn't trust her. That she was relying on him too much. That restless feeling creeping up on her grated on raw nerves and pacing inside the villa wasn't helping. Instead, she looked out across the pool and knew where she wanted to go.

As she entered the pretty wildflower meadow she was greeted by the red thumbprints of poppies bobbing and weaving across the tall grasses, reminding her of the finger paintings that her sister would bring back from the children's ward. Soft smudges of purples and cornflower blue, crested on the waves of gentle colours that called to her and softened her fears.

She lost track of time, just enjoying the simplicity of being here, until she found a rocky outcrop that nudged at her memory. It wasn't far from the section of land that belonged to Gianni, but she had known it would be there somehow and it unsettled her. She looked around, mentally drawing the boundaries of the land she had traversed, and her pulse began to thud heavily in her heart.

She knew this land.

She had seen it in drawings, and paperwork and a folder that had her father's name on it. And the realisation horrified her because finally she knew what it meant. Not just for the past, but for her future.

CHAPTER TWELVE

IT WAS LATER than Alessandro had hoped, but finally they were beginning to make headway on the problems that had stalled the Aurora project. Sofia Obeid had been impressive and as dedicated as he had been throughout the tense renegotiation with their contractors. Bitterly, he had to agree with Obeid; it would have been much quicker if they'd had Amelia on board, but he had dismissed the suggestion without excuse. Because how could he tell Sofia why he had cut Amelia out, when he couldn't even explain it to himself? Still. What was done was done and all he wanted to do was sink into a soft bed, and find that blessed oblivion only Amelia could offer him.

It was dusk by the time he returned to the villa, the sun reluctantly loosening its grip on the day. But Amelia wasn't in the house. He searched the rooms, not yet worried until she saw that the sliding door to the garden was open.

He marched towards the pool, concern sweeping through him like a wave, images of Amelia fainting again, of being in trouble and out of his reach, flung through his mind like sea spray. He gathered his speed and couldn't resist the urge to call out. Her name echoed in the vast area of the sprawling estate and something twisted in him at how lonely and desolate it sounded.

He rounded the corner to find her standing at the edge of the wildflower meadow, relief cutting through him to reveal a thread of heated anger, now that fear was edging from his system.

'Didn't you hear me calling?' he demanded as he reached closer to where she stood.

She turned to pin him with a gaze that nearly stopped him in his tracks.

Accusations, hurt and anger simmered there and he felt as if he had stepped back in time, as if they belonged on the face of a woman who wasn't yet carrying his child. He looked between her and the field and realised that she knew, that somehow she had figured it out.

'This is the land my father sold you.'

He wanted to curse. He wanted to deny it. He'd known that this moment would come and yet he'd prayed it wouldn't. Finally he nodded, watching her warily, as if suddenly she had become a great threat to him. And she was. In some ways that was exactly what she was. Ever since Hong Kong, she had changed him, had him thinking things, feeling things, remembering things—none were welcome and none were wanted. *Cristo*, he should have been able to resolve the issues they'd had on the Aurora project with the click of his fingers, but no, it had taken three days, because of her.

'You kept it.'

'Yes.'

'Well, let's face it. You did more than just keep it,' she said, her tone heavy with a cynicism he didn't recognise in her.

He frowned.

'Really?' she demanded. 'You aren't that clueless, Alessandro. You are self-aware enough to know what you were doing.'

The taunt cut deep. 'Of course I knew what I was doing. Gianni and I made the decision the moment we could afford to,' he bit out. 'We built our homes around that one moment of betrayal so that we would never forget. *Never.* So that we would know the value of our hard work, and know that the only people we could trust was ourselves.'

She shook her head as if horrified by his words. 'This is more than my father,' she said, needling out the truth from him against his will. 'This is deeper than that.'

He reached for her instinctively—and she pulled away. He fisted the outstretched hand that dropped to his side.

'I need to know,' she said, her words barely audible in the gentle buzz and flutter of night-time wildlife. In the dusk he saw her place a hand over where their child grew within her and Alessandro knew she was right.

'To know what?'

'If you are capable of forgiveness. If there is even the slightest bit of hope for our future. You wake up every morning and look out at *this*,' she said, gesturing to the field behind her. 'You force yourself to hold onto that bitterness, to that symbol of betrayal. Is this how you feel about your mother?' she asked, her words hitting him like bullets in the chest, her eyes shining like diamonds in the darkness, her tears for him hurting more than he could possibly say.

'She betrayed us.' He slashed his hand through the air as if cutting off any more conversation. 'I know she tried the best she could,' he forced out, his heart and his hurt at war as it always had been. 'I know that she loves me—and Gianni too. And I love her too. So much that it hurts. But she still betrayed us.'

'Alessandro,' Amelia said, shaking her head helplessly, not knowing what to say. 'What happened to you was devastating. It was so wrong and I am truly sorry,' she said, hoping that he would hear the sincerity in her words. Her heart broke for him, for the child he had never been allowed to be. But that hurt made her even more sure that what she was doing was right. 'You have never forgiven her?' she dared to ask.

His silence was a knife to her heart. And now it was breaking for her, as the flame of hope she'd nurtured in his absence had just been snuffed out.

'Will you ever forgive *me*?' she asked, refusing to be cowed by the question. Her words rang into the night, clear and true. And she saw it—in his eyes—the past, his pain, his demons, all rising in the shadows around him.

'Amelia, you are pushing this too far too fast,' he warned her. And he was right, because she *was* pushing this too fast—even as she knew she shouldn't, but she couldn't stop herself from throwing them towards an impossible conclusion. Because if she didn't, she would only watch him walk away from her again and again and again. She was never going to be enough for him, just as she hadn't been enough for either of her parents.

'Does it matter?' she asked.

'Yes,' he said, sincerely. 'It does. I need time. Please…'

But she couldn't give him that, she thought, even as she knew she was wrong to refuse him it. The idea of watching another person in her life give up on her was too much. She had given her heart to him and he was already shutting her out because he didn't trust her. It rocked her to be standing here in the proof of how adamantly he clung to his betrayals.

'You won't forgive me, will you?' she said, her heart shattering beneath his gaze. 'It's why you kept the problems with Aurora from me, because you can't trust me.'

It was as if he'd been turned to stone, her statement proved truer for it. The only reason she knew he was still alive was the breath sawing in and out of his chest.

'Yet you trust me with your child?' she asked, half terrified, her breath caught in her lungs, because if he didn't—

'Yes.'

The word burst from his lips and she knew, instinctively, that he was telling the truth. She was thankful for it, but it wasn't enough.

'I need more than that, and our child does too.' She needed to know that their child would be raised in love and support without bitter undercurrents that dragged unformed hearts under.

He flinched. She barely caught it in the shadows of a night descending relentlessly, as if time was—and had always been—running out for them. And he simply stared at her while their lives began to come apart at the seams. Everything she'd hoped for, wished for in the sweetest of dreams, was falling away and he was doing nothing to stop it.

'Say something, damn you,' she hurled at him.

'There is nothing left to say.' His voice was raw as if he'd struggled to say even that.

'Yes, there is,' she said, her voice now shaking with a hurt and devastation that was only just beginning. 'You lied to me, Alessandro. You told me that you would keep me safe, you would protect me. You cling so tightly to others' betrayal, but it's you. *You* are the one who betrayed me, this time, Alessandro. *You* are guilty of that.'

And with that, she stalked past him and returned to the house, every step dimming the hope that he might stop her until it was snuffed out completely with the message that dinged her phone.

The jet is at your disposal.

* * *

Amelia hadn't been surprised to find a car waiting for her by the time she came downstairs with her clothes all packed in her suitcase. She'd been tempted to leave the things he had bought for her in Orvieto behind, but stubborn and stupid were close enough and it was possible she would need the clothes before long.

She knew that Alessandro would give her whatever she needed. He would never turn his back on her or their child. There would be painful, difficult, stilted conversations to come, but all she needed, right now, was time, space and...*her sister*.

She wanted to go home. But as the private jet swept in the arc that would bring them down to the English runway, she knew that the flat she shared with her sister just wasn't it. Home was where the heart was and she had just left that in Italy in the keeping of a man who was so determined to protect himself, he might never understand the value of what she'd given him.

She was holding herself together with numb fingers and desperation when she received a text message, and then another and then another. Hope turned to ash the moment she caught her sister's name on the phone's screen and she hated herself for being disappointed that it wasn't Alessandro.

Are you okay?

I'm back.

Where are you?

I don't know, her mind cried in reply. Amelia didn't have a plan for this. And for the first time in her life she wanted to give up, to curl up in a ball, to howl her pain as her mother had, to lose herself as her father had. But she couldn't. She had a little life to protect and, as much as her fragile heart was fractured and breaking, she needed to get up. She needed to make a plan. She needed to be the strong one.

Issy's name flashed up on the screen a second before her phone started to ring. Evidently her sister was too impatient to wait any longer.

'Issy?'

'Oh, my God, Amelia. Oh, thank God. Are you okay? Where are you?'

Amelia struggled to respond, wanting to tell her, wanting to give her answers to her questions, wanting to explain so much more, wanting to beg for forgiveness for lying to her about the evidence of corruption, for putting her in jeopardy with Gianni, for ruining her childhood on some naïve and mistaken path of vengeance. But instead, all she was capable of saying was her sister's name, before a sob took over and the tears came and they wouldn't stop.

In some distant part of her mind she knew she was on the verge of hysteria, that she needed to stop, pull herself together, but she just couldn't. It wasn't just Alessandro, it was her mother, her father, it was all of it and she couldn't keep it in any more. It was pouring out of her and nothing would make it stop.

Then she felt hands come around her. Small hands, but strong arms and she looked up to find Issy staring at her, tears in her own eyes, and concern stark across her features.

'Lia, please. You're okay. It's okay, I promise. It will all be okay,' her younger sister said, smoothing damp tendrils of hair away from her hot wet face.

Amelia didn't even think to ask how Issy had found her on a private jet on a runway in England. She didn't think to feel shame or embarrassment about what the staff had witnessed or where they were. She just let her sister envelop her, let herself sink into her sister's loving embrace and let that feeling heal and soothe just enough to get through the next minute and the minute after.

'I'm so sorry, Issy. I'm so, so sorry.'

'Shh. You have nothing to be sorry for. Nothing,' her sister said with such vehemence, it nearly made Amelia smile.

As her jagged breathing slowed and eased, she looked up and saw Issy for the first time. The Caribbean had glazed her skin golden, the blonde of her hair actually suiting her. 'Issy, you look beautiful.'

'Thank you,' she said, a simple shoulder shrug accepting the compliment without deflection or dismissal and it was lovely to see. 'You, however, Lia, look bloody awful.'

Amelia barked out a laugh and something eased in

her chest. 'Oh, Issy. I've made such a mess of things,' she said, the sadness returning as swiftly as the flutter of a bird's wings.

'Whatever it is, we will fix it,' Issy replied confidently, and Amelia relished the feeling of being comforted, of being cared for. Issy turned to look behind her at the man standing at the top of the cabin.

Amelia's heart lurched, the height and breadth so similar to Alessandro it had fooled her for a moment. But then she saw all the ways in which Gianni Rossi was different from his cousin, one of them being the sheer love she saw when he looked at her sister.

Something unspoken passed between them and Issy turned back to her and asked, 'Can you come with us? I want to take you home.'

And even though the word jarred, even though Amelia was sure her sister didn't mean back to the one-bedroom flat in Brockley, even though she nodded and let herself be gently taken from the cabin of the private jet, she knew that wherever she was going it wasn't home, because Alessandro wouldn't be there.

For the next few weeks Alessandro stayed at Villa Vittoria, taking complete control of the Aurora project. He saw every email, every message, every report—it all went through him. And he knew that he was behaving like a tyrant, but somehow it had become imperative that nothing go wrong on this project. That nothing caught him by surprise again.

Gianni had tried to talk to him when he'd returned from the Caribbean, but for the first time in his life Alessandro didn't want to talk to his cousin. Just seeing the happiness Gianni had found with Isabelle Seymore, of all people, was unbearable and he *hated* that he felt that way. Never had he been jealous or resentful of the cousin who was more like a brother to him, but Gianni's joy came too soon after the sheer shock of Amelia's departure from his life.

You're hiding. I understand that. But it can only last so long.

But Gianni was wrong. Alessandro could make it last as long as he needed it to. Technology allowed him to stay in Tuscany and only fly out when necessary for meetings in both Europe and on the African continent should Sofia Obeid need it.

If she had noticed anything different about his exchanges, she had said nothing. Nor had she mentioned Amelia once. Which, instead of soothing his curiosity, only made it worse as he wondered if they were in communication, wondered if they spoke regularly, or at all.

He was not that surprised when he received the first message from Amelia informing him of her obstetrician's details. Of the first appointment. Of the results of the first scan. He hated himself for answering each message with one-word answers, but he wasn't capable of more. Because he would trail off into explanations, or justifications or demands that she return to him, or pleas that she let him return to her. And he wasn't ready for that. He knew that. *Recognised* that. Because she'd been right. He was still stuck in the past, its grip a vice around his heart and soul holding him in a place where he was not worthy of a future with Amelia and his child. Not yet.

He knew what it looked like from the outside…that he'd abandoned everything, including the mother of his unborn child, but he had never—*would* never do that. He had sent Amelia access to an account just for her that was separate from an account for their child. He had sent her the paperwork that showed he had no access to that account, would not be able to see any expenditures or receive notifications, knowing that it was the least he could do.

The only person he saw, aside from Gianni or Sofia in the occasional meeting he attended, was his mother. As the weeks turned into months, he began to travel to Milan almost once a week. The first time he'd visited it had been intensely painful. He had been full of resentment, anger and hurt. He hadn't expected much, he hadn't even really expected to talk, but his mother had appeared relieved, as if she'd been waiting for this day to come. That time they had simply, and very awkwardly, made polite conversation. Aurora Vizzini hadn't questioned him, asked him why he was there, or pushed him beyond what he was capable of, which was probably for the best. If she had, he might have left and not come back.

On the third visit they'd argued, impatience getting

the better of him, hurt taking over, but as he'd left, she'd told him that she loved him. On the fifth visit he'd told her about Amelia and on the seventh he finally asked why they hadn't left that night. Why—when he and Gianni had needed to leave so badly—had she stayed?

Sitting in the chair, she couldn't meet his gaze. 'The shame and guilt that I couldn't be strong enough for you and Gianni…it will never leave. The horror that I allowed that man to inflict upon you…' She trailed off, shadows haunting her gaze.

And that was when his hurt and anger welled up to the surface, only to be swept back down in a whirlpool of guilt and anguish. 'But what about what he inflicted upon you? I couldn't stop it, Mamma,' he said, his voice quiet, but as rough as if he'd been howling his pain for years. Hot damp heat pressed against his eyes. 'I couldn't stop him, Mamma,' he repeated uselessly.

'You were a child, Alessandro, of course you couldn't stop it.'

'But I wasn't always—I grew, I was—'

'No, *mio bambino*, it was not for you to protect me. I was…glad when he realised that he could no longer… behave the way he had done.'

The anger and frustration that Alessandro had felt, once he had become bigger than his father and the physical threats had lessened but the manipulations and constant mental abuse had increased. And still he'd been powerless to do anything until they'd been old enough to escape, to get out, find jobs and work to support themselves—to support her.

'I couldn't get us out sooner,' he replied, the hot, furious energy leaving him utterly drained, as if he'd run a marathon.

'You got us out,' his mother stated, her eyes full of vehemence, determined that he would see how much that meant to her. *It is more than I did,* came the silent conclusion. 'I am so sorry for what I was unable to do as your mother.'

He shook off her apologies and she snatched up his hand, her skin silky soft and paper thin, her age startling to him as if only moments ago she'd been a young woman at the mercy of her husband.

'You need to hear it, know it and believe it. I am sorry that I could not protect you.'

'And I am sorry for exactly the same thing,' he replied, all that anger, all that hot rage melting away beneath the realisation that it was never about betrayal. It was never about being let down or lied to...it was about the helplessness that he'd felt as a child that had stifled and terrified him.

All these years he'd thought that he'd got up and got out, all these years he'd taken pride in his determination and ability to succeed, to strive forward, move on, but he was still there. Amelia had been right. He was still locked in the past, in his body, unable to escape—because *he* was the trap he had made for himself. *His* were the chains that roped his body and his mind and his heart.

It's you. You *are the one who betrayed me, this time, Alessandro.* You *are guilty of that.*

And in that moment, he realised how truly he had messed things up and finally he broke. The invincible shields he'd drawn around himself shattered all at once, falling to the floor, leaving him vulnerable and weak. And this time he allowed his mother to wrap her arms around him and protect him.

CHAPTER THIRTEEN

Three months later...

AMELIA FOLDED HER jumper and placed it in the suitcase
beside the bed in the spare room of Gianni's penthouse
apartment in London as her sister, Issy, hovered anx-
iously in the corner. She couldn't help but feel the pull
of a smile tugging at her lips, knowing that her sister
wouldn't stay silent for long.

'Don't go,' she begged.

'Issy.' Amelia turned and smiled. 'It's not far.'

'It's the other side of the river!' Issy cried.

'It's fifteen minutes away,' Amelia said, setting free
the gentle thread of laughter beneath her words. Issy's
eyes, though, were full of concern—a concern that
Amelia understood. When Issy had first found her, she
had been utterly devastated. Full of heartache, not only
for the future she had lost with Alessandro, but the past
she had lost because of her parents.

The first month she had spent with the new and de-
lightfully happy couple had been hard in many ways.

The conversations that she'd had with Issy about their parents had been honest, difficult, but ultimately deeply healing. And they were conversations she wouldn't have had, had Alessandro not initially allowed her to come into those feelings in a safe space.

She resisted the urge to check her phone. Usually, he was quick with his one-word responses to her messages about her obstetrics appointments, but uncharacteristically he hadn't messaged in reply to her last one.

'Are you sure you're ready? I mean, you can always stay here a little longer?'

'Don't you want the place to yourself with your new husband?' Amelia asked.

'God, yes, but, oh—I'm sorry!' Issy had a hand pressed to her mouth, clearly worried about what Amelia would think, but she needn't have worried.

'Never be sorry, Is! Never. I'm thrilled for you,' Amelia said, wrapping her arms around her little sister and holding on tight. 'Really. But it's time that I got used to doing this on my own.'

Understanding shone in her sister's eyes, before she heard Gianni calling for her below. With a quick kiss to her cheek, Issy left Amelia alone in the lovely room that had been a haven for her when she most needed it. Her heart turned in her chest as she wondered about Alessandro, worried about what haven he had gone to after she had returned to England.

Over and over again she had replayed their conversation in her mind, seeing at almost every turn where she had gone wrong, but been unable to stop herself from doing so. She despised herself for not being able to give him what he'd needed when he—who had rarely ever asked anything for himself—had asked for it. She'd wanted to, but she'd been so battered and bruised, having only just accepted the damage from her parents, it had not been within her power.

Amelia had found a female counsellor in North London in the second month, knowing that she had many things to work on in order not to make the same mistakes as her parents when it came to raising her child. She would accept whatever help in whatever form to provide her child with the best that she could possibly give, and that had—she reluctantly realised—included dipping into the account that Alessandro had provided for her.

She needed her own space to think and to be. Looking back now, the unease she had felt, the desperation that had driven her to force Alessandro's hand, what had shaped so much of those last days with him, had been fear. Fear that had teeth and claws from the neglect of her parents who had left her alone carrying a burden that was too much for a young teenager. But she wasn't that scared young teenager any more. She was an adult now, who relished the chance to care for her child, to accept that responsibility not as a burden but as a gift.

Now she could see that she wanted to share her life with Alessandro because she loved him, because she admired him, because he was exactly the kind of man her father had never been to his family—but most importantly Amelia knew that she didn't *need* him to be the parent she wanted to be and the woman she knew she already was.

Her heart hurt to recognise it, but her soul knew it was right. As right as her need to find the right way to truly apologise to him. But for the first time, where Alessandro was concerned, she didn't have a plan. A fix. Something that she could prepare for. Only…she knew that she wanted to apologise. Because for all her accusations of betrayal, she *was* the one who had let him down when he had needed her understanding the most.

Alessandro knocked on the door, unease painting thick strokes of ice across his back. When Gianni opened the door, he caught surprise, shock, hurt all flit across his cousin's gaze, before it was replaced with indifference—a look Alessandro had never thought to see on Gianni's face. But he could concede that it was the least he deserved.

Ever since Amelia had left Villa Vittoria, he'd been acting like a stranger. After the painful confrontation with his mother, Alessandro had completely retreated. He'd handed over control of the project to the team with final oversight going to Gianni and Sofia. He'd left Italy and its memories so that he could have the time and space to think clearly about what he wanted for his child, what he wanted for himself, and what he wanted for Amelia.

Looking back on it, he could see how badly the lie about Firstview had sat with Amelia. The shadows beneath her eyes, her behaviour stilted and pained, until the truth had come out. And then her fierce love and protection for her sister, her determination to make it right, her adamant protection of their child and her desperate desire to give their child more than they had… it overwhelmed him.

He didn't just lust after her, that wasn't the connection that had formed between them—as he'd tried to convince himself early on. It was *her*. He loved her. He was inspired by her, awed by her. She was greater than him in every way and he missed her so much it was as if part of him had gone. A part he'd never known existed.

'Are you waiting for an invitation?' Gianni demanded as he beckoned him into the London apartment he was now sharing with his new wife. Isabelle Seymore had taken Gianni's surname and was now Isabelle Rossi and Alessandro was still wrapping his head around how the two cousins had fallen so deeply in love with the daughters of their one-time enemy.

'You!'

The hurled accusation from the living room where a woman who resembled Amelia was pointing at him as if she had accused him of being the murderer in a country house crime drama.

'You!' she repeated.

'Yes, me,' Alessandro replied in the hope that ac-

knowledging it might make her stop—his hands might
have also gestured surrender.

This, he knew, he also deserved.

She glared at him and he knew he'd made a mistake.

'You think this is funny?' she demanded.

'There is nothing funny about it,' he replied truthfully and something in his tone must have made her
stop, as she glanced uncertainly at Gianni who, he saw,
shrugged.

'What do you want?' Isabelle asked, eyeing him with
a considerable amount of suspicion.

'I want to know where Amelia is.'

Isabelle snorted and he thought he'd heard her say,
yeah, not likely, but he couldn't be sure. He looked at
Gianni.

'I need to see her.'

Gianni shook his head. 'You are my cousin—my
blood. But she is my wife. You'll understand one day.'

'Not if no one tells me where Amelia is,' he all but
growled, his frustration getting the better of him.

'You broke her heart,' Isabelle accused.

'I know,' Alessandro admitted.

'No. You don't. She is my sister and I will fight to the
death for her and her child,' she said fiercely and suddenly he saw it—the similarity between the siblings, the
passion, the fire, the determination. 'You—' she stabbed
a finger at him '—broke—' another stab '—her.'

'And I promise you that—if I get the chance—I will
spend every single day for the rest of my life ensuring

that it never happens again. I know that nothing I say will fix the damage that has been done, but she needs to know that it was *me*, not her.' His words burned and cracked as they came from his soul, but he needed to say them. '*I* caused the cracks that broke a strong, powerful, beautiful woman,' he said, thumping his chest. 'I need her to know that,' he said to Isabelle, his tone all but begging.

Something flickered across Isabelle's gaze and he felt the hairs stand on the back of his neck. He felt the pull of that connection that he only ever felt when Amelia was nearby. He turned, slowly, vaguely registering Gianni pulling his wife from the room, because all he saw was Amelia. Amelia glowing, eyes bright, cheeks flushed healthily and skin still wearing the faint bronze of Italy. Amelia so round with their child that it took his breath away.

'You're here?' Alessandro couldn't believe his eyes.

'Yes, I… I wanted to be with family,' she said, unable to meet his gaze.

He took a step forward, but the way that Amelia held herself made him stop. She looked as if she were trying to hold the pieces of herself together and he hated that he'd done this to her. But he bore it, because that was his due.

'You heard what I said to your sister?' he asked, his words sounding as if they'd been dragged across gravel.

Amelia nodded, sending a wave of chestnut rippling

down her back. Her hair was longer, richer, more vibrant than he remembered.

'It was not… I wanted to…' Alessandro bit back a curse. He'd planned what he'd wanted to say to her, how he wanted to start, and this was going horribly wrong. He wasn't prepared, but that didn't, couldn't matter. She deserved to know and hear the truth of his feelings and he needed to tell them. He took a breath—a deep one.

'You make me flustered,' he admitted, helplessly. 'And I don't get flustered. At least not any more. My mother tells me that it used to happen to me as a child when I desperately wanted something,' he said, ruefully, rubbing the back of his neck.

'*Tells* you?' Amelia asked, picking up on the tense he had used.

He nodded. 'We've been spending some time together,' he replied, noticing the way her hand had begun to sweep slow, soothing circles over her round belly. He wondered if she'd felt their baby kick.

'I went to see her. You were right—about so many things. But the first and most important one was how trapped I was by the past. How it coloured everything and made it impossible for me to move on, move forward with any kind of life, let alone one that I want more than my next breath.' He hoped that she could read the truth in his gaze—that it was a life with her that he was speaking of.

Amelia was standing by the large window looking out onto the street as if only partially listening to him, but he knew—he knew that all of her considerable focus was on him. He felt it like a touch—warm, comforting, hopeful.

'I realised that it was not her I was angry with,' he said, willingly offering Amelia the deepest of his truths, baring his soul to her, hoping that somehow he might be worthy of her, 'it was me.' Some of the shame he had spent years wrapped in still lingered, but he was working through that knowing that neither he nor his mother deserved to feel shame or anger any more.

Amelia turned to him at his words. 'Alessandro—' She reached for him and he went to her, but he also needed to finish. As if she had read the thought in his mind, she held her words back.

'There is much more work I need to do, she and I need to do, but all this time I thought that I had left the past behind me and you were right. I was chained by it. And had it not been for you I would never have seen that, never have realised it. No matter what happens after today, or in any of the days that follow, I want you to know that you have changed my life for the better because of who you are. And I love you.'

Amelia's heart quivered, little gentle shakes rippling throughout her body.

'I love you,' Alessandro said again, as if he knew that she needed to hear it. 'And I will never stop loving you.'

She reached a hand to the chair to hold herself up. 'And I know that I offered you the security you wanted with one hand, and took it away with the other—the security to know that you were safe and loved and trusted—and I will never forgive myself for that.'

Amelia wondered if his words were magic, summoning all the broken shards of herself, raising them from the ground and bringing them back together. She wanted desperately to speak, to share of herself in the same way that he was, but she held herself back because she knew that he needed to say this. They had time, she began to realise with an expansion of her heart. They could take this time not to rush.

'I understand,' Alessandro continued, 'if you choose to move forward on your own with our child. I would...' His words stumbling once again, letting her know how hard this was for him, how much he struggled with what he wanted and letting her go to have what she wanted. 'I would like to be involved in my child's life,' he said, her heart cracking, but not breaking, reforming anew rather than what it had been like before, reforming to make room for him, right beside the love she felt for their child. 'But I trust that you know what is best for our child,' Alessandro said, and even the thought of him retreating, of him removing himself from their lives, cut her to the quick.

Finally, as if on the brink of his retreat, she found the courage to move towards what she wanted with her whole entire being.

'Alessandro,' she said, closing the distance between them and taking his face in her hands. 'I'm so sorry,' she said. The surprise in his gaze would have been near funny if it weren't so sad. 'I'm so sorry,' she repeated uselessly. Months of planning what she would say and her heart simply beat too loudly for her to hear what she had hoped to have the chance to say.

'I was so scared. I saw you retreating into work, shutting me out, which,' she said, holding up her hand to stop him from explaining, 'I understand, utterly and completely. It was what you needed to do in that moment. How *could* you have included me after I nearly destroyed your company? But I used that to feed fears I barely knew I had. I panicked and just couldn't see how you would want to stay with me when…when even my parents hadn't. But I'm working on that, and on much more,' she said, wanting to share the decisions she had made in the last few months, wanting to share so much of *her* life with him, not just their child's.

'I love you,' she said, her words overwhelmed by the depth of her emotions. 'I love you—powerful, proud, driven and occasionally flustered, you. The you who is loyal, caring, protective and who wears that love for his family on his sleeve.' His eyes exploded with hope, starbursts alight with love and want and the infinity that she had thought she had found with him once before.

He took a sharp breath, as if shocked by her declaration, and gently pressed his forehead against hers as if in reverence.

'If you take me back, I promise you'll not regret it. I'll

spend every single day proving myself worthy of you.'
He pulled back enough to look her in the eye.

'If you take me back, I promise to spend each and
every day showing you the love and family that you are
worthy of a hundred times over,' she said with a vehemence that matched the man she loved.

Her lips found his, and everything she'd ever wanted
was in that kiss: Love, reverence, security, and everything she wanted to give him, she desperately hoped
he felt. But when she wrapped her arms around him to
pull him against her, something poked into her ribs.
Angling back, and reluctantly breaking the kiss, she
pressed her hands to his chest.

'What is…?'

Alessandro reached into his jacket inner pocket, a
flush riding his cheeks.

'I've been carrying this with me for the last two
months,' he said, and although there were nerves in
his gaze, there was a dizzying anticipation. He pulled
a small blue velvet box from his jacket. 'After all the
mistakes I made, there will never be a right time. I know
that. But I had hoped to at least do this properly,' he explained as he lowered himself to one knee.

Her hands flew to her mouth, stifling the gasp that
caught on a smile. He opened the box to reveal a ring
so perfect it could have been made for her. It had small
green sapphire stones around a perfect red ruby, and
it reminded her of the wildflower meadow at the heart
of Alessandro's home.

'Amelia Seymore, you are the better part of my world, the whole of my life, and the only future I could ever have. I love you in a way that makes me better, that makes me want to be better and that brings me hope every single day. Will you do me the greatest honour, and be my lover, my partner, my companion so that I can love you, protect you and be with you for the rest of my days?'

Tears gathered in her eyes, and she happily shed them to see the shining love in his gaze for her.

'Yes,' she said, nodding. 'Oh, yes, please,' she added, pulling him from the floor so that she could embrace him. 'I love you, Alessandro Rossi,' she said, before placing her lips across his, and finally, after what felt like years of searching, Amelia Seymore came *home*.

EPILOGUE

'*CARA*, PLEASE, YOU'RE DOING it all wrong—*ouch*!' Alessandro exclaimed as his wife slapped his hand away from the meal she was trying to prepare. It wasn't the slapping hand that worried him, but the knife gripped in the other that he eyed warily.

'Mr Rossi. I have six years of experience when it comes to making our daughter's favourite meal. Would you care to argue the same?'

The look in his eyes plainly told her he could, but instead he said, 'I would care not to argue at all, Mrs Rossi, but if you insist, perhaps we can take this into the other room?' The innocent expression on his face was utterly obliterated by the heady desire pouring from his gaze.

His hand slipped around her back and pulled her as close to him as her eight-month baby bump would allow. As much as Amelia wanted to, and she really did, Issy and Gianni and their children were due over soon and so much still needed to be done.

It had been nearly six months since she'd last seen

them, her current pregnancy had been a little difficult and had prevented her from flying over to the Caribbean Island Issy and Gianni spent half of the year on, and she was desperately looking forward to seeing her sister.

Amelia looked across the counter top to the large wooden table set for their entire family. She remembered once imagining Alessandro sitting at it all alone and it pleased her to know that she had never seen that come to reality. As her husband tried to distract her with kisses to her neck—his favourite place on her body, it seemed—she remembered with a full heart the Christmases, New Years, birthdays, and every celebration they could make, shared with family and laughter and love.

'They would understand,' he whispered seductively in her ear. 'They're worse than we are. At it like rabbits, as you English like to say.'

'Mamma, what are rabbits "at"?' their daughter, Hope, asked innocently from the other side of the kitchen counter appearing—as usual—from nowhere. Hope Rossi had inherited her parents' ferocious intelligence and her love of books from her paternal grandmother, if Aurora Vizzini's proclamation was anything to go by.

'Jumping. Running and jumping around the meadow,' Amelia replied without missing a beat while Alessandro choked on his shocked laugh.

'The one where we meet Uncle Gianni and Auntie Issy and Mia and Matteo for picnics when they're home?'

Amelia nodded. She wondered just how much her niece and nephew would have grown as Alessandro swept up their daughter in his arms and threw her into the air, catching her without even raising Amelia's blood pressure. He had kept true to the promise he had made, not only the day he proposed, but before then, in a café in Orvieto. He had kept them safe, he had given them everything they could have even wished for, let alone needed.

And she had never, in the days and years that followed, questioned his love and unconditional support. She'd had it when she had chosen to work with Sofia Obeid, at first part time after her maternity leave and then full time as partner in Sofia's company. And she'd had it while she had explored her issues from her parents with the therapist. Sometimes she still felt the echoes of the past, as she knew Alessandro did, but the healing that had been done with Aurora, who was also set to arrive for his birthday meal shortly, was a beautiful thing to see.

'My love,' he said, gently moving her out of the way of the oven so he could check on the food. It turned out that Alessandro loved nothing more than providing for and feeding his family. A family that would grow again in just one month's time. 'Can you please sit down?' he asked, still concerned about how much she was doing at this stage of her pregnancy. She shot him a glare that had none of the anger of their early interactions and all the heat that had burned between them from the very beginning.

He could see that she was about to argue when Hope heard the chatter of her cousins and the laugh of her uncle and aunt coming from the garden and she was off like a shot, allowing Alessandro to steal a kiss from his beautiful wife. He remembered how he had once been shocked by the possessiveness that had made him fear he had lost his mind. Instead, he realised later, it had been his heart. And only once he'd accepted his love, and had that love returned, had he found a peace and sense of rightness that he had never imagined possible. That didn't mean that they hadn't argued or that there hadn't been hard times to overcome. But they had faced, and would continue to face, each and every challenge together, safe in the knowledge and assurance of their love.

No one looking at them from the outside would have ever believed that they had once been enemies. Enemies who had become lovers and then soulmates bound together for the rest of their days by a love that was true and everlasting.

* * * * *

#4105 THE BABY BEHIND THEIR MARRIAGE MERGER
Cape Town Tycoons
by Joss Wood

After one wild weekend with tycoon Jude, VP Addison must confess a most unprofessional secret...she's pregnant! But Jude has a shocking confession of his own: to inherit his business, he *must* legitimize his heir—by making Addi his bride!

#4106 KIDNAPPED FOR THE ACOSTA HEIR
The Acostas!
by Susan Stephens

One unforgettable night with Alejandro leaves Sienna carrying a nine-month secret! But before she has the chance to confess, he discovers the truth and steals her away on his superyacht. Now, Sienna is about to realize how intent Alejandro is on claiming his child...

#4107 ITALIAN NIGHTS TO CLAIM THE VIRGIN
by Sharon Kendrick

Billionaire Alessio can think of nothing worse than attending another fraught family event alone. So, upon finding Nicola moonlighting as a waitress to make ends meet, they strike a bargain. He'll pay the innocent to accompany him to Italy...as his girlfriend!

#4108 WHAT HER SICILIAN HUSBAND DESIRES
by Caitlin Crews

Innocent Chloe married magnate Lao for protection after her father's death. They've lived separate lives since. So, when she's summoned to his breathtaking Sicilian castello, she expects him to demand a divorce. But her husband demands the opposite— an heir!

HPCNMRA0423

#4109 AWAKENED BY HER ULTRA-RICH ENEMY
by Marcella Bell

Convinced that Bjorn, like all wealthy men, is up to no good, photojournalist Lyla sets out to prove it. But when her investigation leads to an accidental injury, she's stranded under her enemy's exhilarating gaze...

#4110 DESERT KING'S FORBIDDEN TEMPTATION
The Long-Lost Cortéz Brothers
by Clare Connelly

To secure his throne, Sheikh Tariq is marrying a princess. It's all very simple until his intended bride's friend and advisor, Eloise, is sent to negotiate the union. And Tariq suddenly finds his unwavering devotion to duty tested...

#4111 CINDERELLA AND THE OUTBACK BILLIONAIRE
Billionaires of the Outback
by Kelly Hunter

When his helicopter crashes, a captivating stranger keeps Reid alive. Under the cover of darkness, a desperate intimacy is kindled. So, when Reid is rescued and his Cinderella savior disappears, he won't rest until he finds her!

#4112 RIVALS AT THE ROYAL ALTAR
by Julieanne Howells

When the off-limits chemistry that Prince Sebastien and Queen Agnesse have long ignored explodes...the consequences are legally binding! They have faced heartbreak apart. But if they can finally believe that love exists...it could help them face their biggest trial *together*.

HARLEQUIN
PLUS

Try the best multimedia subscription service for romance readers like you!

Read, Watch and Play.

Experience the easiest way to get the romance content you crave.

Start your **FREE TRIAL** at
<u>www.harlequinplus.com/freetrial</u>.